I073456

The Seamus McCree Series
By James M. Jackson

THE NOVELS

Ant Farm
Bad Policy
Cabin Fever
Doubtful Relations
Empty Promises
False Bottom
Granite Oath
Hijacked Legacy

THE NOVELLAS

Furthermore
Low Tide at Tybee

Nonfiction
By Jim Jackson

One Trick at a Time:
How to Start Winning at Bridge

LOW TIDE AT TYBEE

LOW TIDE AT TYBEE

A Seamus McCree Novella

James M. Jackson

Low Tide at Tybee was first published by Wolf's Echo Press as part of *Lowcountry Crimes: Four Novellas* (2017)

Trade Paperback Edition: November 2020

Wolf's Echo Press
PO Box 54
Amasa, MI 49903
www.WolfsEchoPress.com

ISBN-13 Trade Paperback: 978-1-943166-23-7
ISBN-13 Electronic Edition   978-1-943166-11-4

Printed in the United States of America
1098765432

DEDICATION

For beach lovers everywhere

Day One, Monday

A HIGH TIDE RAISES ALL ships; a low tide reveals what's been hidden under all the water. That's especially true at Tybee Island off the coast of Georgia, where average tides are more than seven feet top to bottom. Following high tides, my granddaughter, Megan McCree, preferred to walk the beach looking for new shells. During low tides, playing on hard-packed sand flats that stretch southeast from the island into the channel of Tybee Creek suited her best.

The day we saw the thief was a Monday. Because it was March, Tybee wasn't crowded even on a cloudless day with temperatures well into the seventies. Water temperature was still fifteen degrees cooler: not a problem for a kid Megan's age, a month and a half past her sixth birthday, but darn nippy for an old fart like me. Megan and I had been wading for more than an hour through pools of water left behind after the tide pulled the ocean away from the shore. My feet had become so cold they were numb.

While Megan chased a group of sanderlings across the flats, mimicking both their frenetic steps and their halts to probe the sand for treasures, I used binoculars to spy on a dozen brown pelicans settled on a sandbar south of us. As though an unseen coach blew his whistle, they sprang into the air and glided north in a line, remaining no more than two feet above the water. An occasional lazy wingbeat propelled their glide.

Megan tugged at my shorts. I leaned down and caught the unique scent of suntan lotion.

"Grampa Seamus? I need to tinkle."

I smiled at the lilt in her voice that put a question mark after my name. As a youngster, she had struggled to say it correctly, pronouncing it Say-mus. Now her perfect Shay-mus would make any Irishman proud, especially one like me, born and bred in Boston.

It had only been fifteen minutes since the last time she "really had to go," and we were to meet my mother at the car in twenty minutes. If I could convince Megan to use a blue porta potty we'd pass on the way to the car, I could leave the cold water and warm my feet on the beach sand. "It's time to leave anyway. Can you hold it until we walk back to the car, or—"

She vehemently shook her head and pointed to the ocean. "Now!" She dramatically crossed her legs to prove how desperate the situation was and contorted her face into a pout.

I choked back a laugh at her performance. Maybe she was telling the truth. More likely she wanted the thrill of peeing in the ocean. Again. Grampa Seamus was a rule-breaker in Megan's eyes, and for a girl who had been taught that peeing in swimming pools was a major offense, this was breaking bad. The first time I had suggested it to her, she was aghast until I reminded her that fish and turtles and birds did it all the time.

I used my left elbow to clamp the binoculars to my side and held Megan's hand with my right. The rolling waves were only six-inches high. We waded into the water until it was over her waist. She grabbed my hand with both of hers, leaned back, and squinched her eyes shut.

I averted my head and caught the flash of a northern gannet, its black-tipped wings pressed tightly against its white body, plunge into the ocean. It popped to the surface with a fish in its beak and maneuvered the meal to swallow it head first. I almost fell backward when Megan stood and released the counterbalance of her weight. With a quick step, I steadied myself. She let go of my hand and waded toward shore.

One of my normal steps equaled three or four of hers, especially while we were in water. I had learned to shorten my stride and try to match her two for one. At least she was now tall enough that I didn't have to lean down to hold her hand.

"Grampa Seamus? Does that man want to read my book?" She pointed high up on the dry sand of the beach toward our towels and beach bags.

Megan's eyesight was much sharper than mine, but I had ten-power binoculars. She was right. A guy in navy swim trunks and a gray hoodie squatted next to our stuff, pawing through one of our two bags. I tapped my shorts pockets, felt the outlines of my keys, wallet, and phone.

Bless her heart, Megan thought her books were valuable; but ignoring her love of books, the bag otherwise contained only suntan lotion, Megan's cover-up, my mother's sweater, our shoes, and the towel Mom had used before she went for her daily walk. The second bag was reserved for wet things, like the shovel and buckets Megan had used to create her fairy sand castle.

The guy swiveled his head, as though checking to see if anyone was watching. It was too far away and the light was wrong for me to get a great look at his face. Dark sunglasses, the bill of a black baseball cap poked from under his hoodie, and the sense of a goatee were the only details I could make out.

I yelled, "Hey! You!" Although he probably couldn't hear me, he might have noticed us pointing and me watching him through my binocs. He rose, and with the long strides of a water bug on a smooth lake, headed for the boardwalk exit over the dunes. His flipflops (black?) kicked up sand with each step. Muscular legs turned his step into a bounce once he hit the bridge spanning the dunes. Youthful, I thought.

Megan pulled me forward. "Let's go."

"In a sec, Pumpkin." I followed the guy's progress, hoping he would stop at the top of the dune bridge and look back. He didn't. "All right, kiddo. Last one to our stuff is a rotten egg."

With a high-pitched squeal of delight, Megan took off. Even though we were more than a soccer pitch away from our belongings, she had proved on earlier beach trips that she could run the entire distance. The rippled texture of the sand didn't seem to bother Megan at all, but on cold-deadened feet, the ridges found pressure points with each of my steps. I mentally said, "Eech" and "Ouch" with alternating steps. Even so, I kept pace with her on the exposed sand bar, once pulling just far enough ahead to cause her to let loose another shriek. She broke into a sprint and surged past me.

I let her stay ahead until we reached the sand of the main beach. Its warmth felt good to my frozen feet, although I knew I'd pay with painful tingles once circulation resumed. Sprinting ahead of her, I turned around and ran backwards so I could keep an eye on her while I chanted in a sing-song voice, "Run, run, as fast as you can. You can't catch me, I'm the gingerbread man. I've run away from a little old woman, and a little old man, and I can run away from you, I can!"

When I judged we were a dozen yards away from our belongings, I purposefully tripped in the loose sand above the high tide line. Megan flew past me and flopped onto her towel. "I won! I won!"

I gave her a friendly pat on the head. "You sure did." A quick check of our bags revealed Mom's sweater was on top. I had placed it on the bottom. The guy had definitely rifled through the bags, but I couldn't visualize anything missing.

What had that been about?

ACCORDING TO MY MOTHER, PROMPTNESS, not cleanliness, was next to Godliness. I expected to hear about my transgressions because Megan and I would be a couple of minutes late to the scheduled meet at our rental car. Once we put the sand dunes between us and the ocean, we lost the cooling breeze. A half-block later, sweat began beading on my forehead. My mouth dried out and tasted of salt. Megan soon lagged, a sure sign she was tired. Maybe Mom had slowed her walk due to the heat and she'd be late, too. I could hope.

Megan perked up a little when I promised to stop at Seaside Sweets on the way home to our rented house as a reward for excellent behavior on the beach. My son, Paddy, and his wife, Cindy, would not have approved of a sweet treat so soon before dinner, but Megan was with me, not them, and what did it matter if dessert came before the main meal? The shot of energy was short lived, and with a hanging head, she shuffled her feet on the last few steps to the car.

The sun had baked the car for the three hours we had been at the beach, so it didn't surprise me that even though Mom had her own set of keys, she wasn't sitting in the car. I scanned the few shady spots along the road hoping to conjure the eighty-one-year old. No Mom.

I dumped the bags into the trunk and opened a car door. A blast of superheated air took my breath away. While the car cooled, I led Megan to the shade of a crepe myrtle in a front yard four houses past the car. "We'll wait for your Geema here," I said. I stuck a finger in one ear to block Megan's decision to sing her ABCs and dialed Mom's cell phone. After five rings, my own voice invited me to leave a voicemail for the dialed number.

At eighty, Mom decided she wanted a man's message on her phone. At the beep, I said, "Where the heck are you, Mom? Megan and I expected to meet you at the car. Did I screw up the time? Give me a call. I don't see you in a couple, I'll walk Megan to Seaside Sweets. You remember where it is, right? On Sixteenth Street? Call, okay?"

I knew I was rambling, but talking delayed worrying about everything that might have gone wrong. She was spry and healthy, but she could have fallen, or had a stroke, or heart attack. What would I do with Megan if I had to go to the hospital?

Megan completed the third go-round of her ABCs and was beginning to fidget. Figuring I could buy a little time, I pulled up an app for a spelling game that Megan loved. It presented an image and she had to spell it. The sights and sounds of fireworks rewarded correct answers. If she misspelled a word, the screen shook and the phone buzzed. It was a battery killer, but more importantly it might prevent a Megan meltdown.

While Megan scored fireworks for DOG, CAT, HAT, RED, ROAD, and a bunch of other three- and four-letter words. I paced the sidewalk, keeping one eye on Megan and the other on the direction of my mother's expected arrival. Two doors down from the crepe myrtle, a bee's buzz grabbed my attention and a new shot of dread poured through my veins. Bees darted around the purple azalea from which the sound arose. Mom's EpiPen was sitting at the house. What if a bee stung her? She could be in anaphylactic shock. My chest sympathetically tightened as I imagined her fighting to breathe.

Where was the nearest hospital? Did they have ambulances on Tybee? They must. It was a city. It had a fire department. Savannah had a teaching hospital. EMTs carried epinephrine, didn't they?

Ten minutes passed. Megan would soon tire of the game. Should we drive to the police station and report my mother missing? They would know if there had been an emergency call, right? By now, Mom could be waiting for us at Seaside Sweets. No, she'd call if she got the message—unless she forgot to charge her phone last night? Wait a minute. I was the one who forgot to charge his phone; Mom never did. She did sometimes forget to power on her phone after shutting it down before going to bed. Maybe today was one of those days?

If I drove to the police station rather than call, I could show them her picture from my cell phone. We could drive by Seaside Sweets on the way in case she was waiting for us. "Come on, Megan. Let's hop in the car and look for your Geema."

"Why, Grampa Seamus? She's right there."

Megan pointed to my mother, who was walking up from the beach—the opposite direction from where I expected to see her. Megan skipped down the sidewalk. So much for being tired. What if she knocked my mother down? She didn't. She stopped and carefully wrapped her arms around my mother's legs in an enthusiastic hug. I was becoming such a worrywart. It was exhausting. I needed a nap.

Hand-in-hand, the two of them ambled toward the car. Once Mom was close enough I didn't have to shout, I said, "I was worried."

"I was afraid of that," Mom said. "I went to take a picture and discovered I had dropped my phone somewhere. I retraced my steps to try to find it. I was darned near three-quarters of the way back when I decided I had left it in the pocket of my sweater. I didn't have any way to contact you."

I clicked the key fob and popped the trunk. "Grab it. Then we need to take Pumpkin for a gelato. I know, it's almost dinner time. But, you were the one late . . ."

Mom grabbed her sweater and patted the pockets. "Maybe it fell out?" She felt around inside the bag.

"I'll call it, so we can follow the sound," I said. A corner of my mind wondered why I hadn't heard it ring when I had called and left the message.

"Good thought," Mom said, "but I turned it off driving to the beach."

"Geema, let's go get ice cream." Megan tugged on my mother's arm and nearly dropped my cell phone.

"Megan," I said to Geema's little helper. "Can you find Geema's phone in the bag? And give me mine while you're looking." To my mother, I added, "You sure you left it with your sweater? You checked your fanny pack, right?"

She gave me a look that said, "How stupid do you think I am?"

"Butter blindness," I said. "You know, you look in the refrigerator for the butter and can't see it right in front of your eyes?"

"Good recovery, Seamus. Look for yourself." She unclasped the fanny pack and handed it to me. "Any luck, sweetie?" she said to Megan.

Megan had dumped the beach bag contents into the trunk and carefully checked each item before stuffing it into the bag. I unzipped the front pocket of the fanny pack where Mom normally kept her phone and recovered lip balm, two pouches of ready-to-use wipes, clip-on sunglasses, and a ballpoint pen from a local real estate office. The larger compartment contained only her flat wallet, Kindle Paperwhite, and darts' case. Mom maintained an enthusiastic following in the world of competition darts. She'd retired from tournament play, but still raised thousands for charities, and she always carried the case with her. My father had given it to her more than forty-five years ago, shortly before he had been killed. It was her personal talisman.

"No phone." Megan emphatically shook her head.

"It's not in with the beach toys?" Mom asked.

"Nope," I said, "but you can check in case I'm the one with butter blindness."

"Oh dear, it was almost brand new. And they're so expensive. Do you think we should try walking the beach once more?"

"No, Mom. I think we saw a guy steal it."

"STOLEN CELL PHONES SEEM TO go in spurts," Tybee Island's Detective Sergeant Brittney Issa said with a dollop of southern drawl in response to our report of the probable theft of Mom's cell phone. "You're the third person in the last two weeks. At least y'all didn't store any confidential data on yours. Sometimes we're lucky and they show up in a lost and found. Sometimes they're used for a day or two and pitched away. You're the first who saw anything. Although white male, medium height, fit, and wearing swimming trunks and a hoodie, doesn't exactly narrow the suspect pool a whole lot. Anything else specific?"

I pegged the detective in her early forties with shrewd eyes behind a friendly demeanor. All the time her words suggested it was a lost cause, she beamed an appreciative smile. Even though I had the feeling her smile was the syrup to catch unwary insects, I liked it a lot better than the tough cop approach some officers take. "I might recognize the way he walked if I saw him again," I said. "But even through the binocs, we were a long way away. Wore dark glasses. Had a goatee. Flip-flops. He might have had a tattoo on his . . ." I closed my eyes to try to conjure the picture. ". . . right leg."

"Spider web." Megan stuck another scoop of strawberry gelato into her mouth and smacked her lips in audible delight.

"Really?" I said. "You could see from so far away?" I gave the detective an eye roll to indicate my skepticism.

Megan dramatically shook her head. "Before."

With that single word, she grabbed our attention. Oblivious to our stares, she concentrated on scraping the last of the gelato from the cup.

"Before what?" I prompted.

"At my fairy castle."

Behind my eyes came a warning throb. "He was at your fairy castle?"

A nod. "He watched me."

"Where was I? Where was Geema?"

"Geema was gone walking. You were watching those big brown birds that crash into the water."

"Pelicans," I said without thinking. *And a man*

approached Megan? "Pretend I was that man. Can you show me how far away he was?"

Megan moved two feet away. Acid burned in my stomach. *That close and I didn't see anything?*

"The spider caught a bug with a green head and big red eye," Megan said.

Detective Sergeant Issa squatted her five and a half feet down to Megan's size. "Did he touch you?"

Head shake.

"Did he talk to you?"

Megan added a "No" to her head shake.

"Can you show me on yourself where it was? The spider?"

Megan pointed to her right calf.

"The spider web was black?" Issa asked.

A nod from Megan.

"Did you recognize the bug? Was it a fly?"

"No!" Megan stomped a foot. "It had a fish tail and no legs. It was stupid. I can draw better, and I can count to a hundred. One, two, three, four, five, six, seven, eight—"

Issa chuckled and returned the eye roll I had given her earlier. "I believe you can, Miss Megan. Now, you look like a smart girl. Can you think hard for me? What else can you tell me?"

To my surprise, Megan did not protest the interruption of her numerical recitation. She squeezed her eyes shut. Her ruby lips flattened. Then her eyes popped open and she pointed to Detective Issa's gun. I held my breath, expecting another revelation about the perpetrator.

"You have a gun. Grampa Seamus doesn't like them, but Geema has one."

"In Boston," my mother quickly added. "With a carry permit. Is there anything else we can do, Detective?"

"I think that's it." Issa rose, signaling an end to our meeting. "I want to again caution you. If your 'find my phone' app kicks up a location, contact us. If you happen to find it yourself, let me know that, too."

Mom looked between us. "Seamus, you're supposed to respond, 'of course.' "

IN THE CAR, MY MOTHER said, "On the way home, let's drive by the place I saw."

"I think I lost a thread, Mom. Which place you saw?"

Mom had fallen in love with Tybee several years earlier once a friend showed it to her. This vacation had multiple purposes: give my son and daughter-in-law a two-week break from child-rearing, let Mom and me spend time alone with Megan, and look for a place I could rent in summers and allow Mom to escape Boston winters.

"The one I wanted to take pictures of when I discovered my phone was missing. It's on our way."

I checked to make sure Megan had secured herself in the car seat. "Okay, a quick drive-by, but we need to feed Megan soon. The ice cream won't hold her for long."

Mom's directions were useless. She had spotted the building on her beach walk and didn't have an address or even an accurate sense of exactly where the building was located other than, "past the pier right on the ocean." After several futile attempts on side streets, I stumbled onto it.

"That one!" Mom proclaimed. "It's the right-most unit of the three-condo building."

I pulled to the curb and powered down the windows for a better look. Three stories high, each unit had a single-car garage underneath the back—clearly inadequate, four vehicles were parked on the lawn and driveway of the left-most unit. The units were narrow with a single rear window on the second and third floors. Sea-green awnings covered each unit's rear entrance and second-floor window. I counted three side windows on the second and third floors and could see the edge of a deck at the second story level.

Topping the building was a red metal roof. The thing had all the charm of a love child between a concrete bunker at Fort Screven, the abandoned coastal fort just down the road, and the metal pole barn building I used for a garage at my place in Michigan's Upper Peninsula.

Yet, it *was* right on the beach. A group of seagulls wheeled overhead, squawking what, after watching *Finding Nemo* with Megan, I would forever think of as, "Mine, Mine, Mine." One of my purchase criteria was to be able to hear waves on the beach at night to lull me to sleep. Even with the current minimal wave action, I picked up the deep thrum of the waves.

A freshening breeze slipping through the gap between buildings brought with it the tang of salt air, fresh even at low tide because the gulls acted as garbage disposals for any dead and rotting fish. It was far enough away from the Tybee pier so the crowds were thinner. It had possibilities.

"I'm cold," Megan complained from the back seat.

The sun was setting behind us and after Megan mentioned it, I realized tingling goosebumps had popped on my bare arms. I raised the windows and looked for a real estate agent sign so I could punch in the property code on my phone and get the particulars. No sign visible. "Did you get a flyer? What are they asking?"

"No clue," Mom said. "A poster in an ocean-side window said it was for sale by owner, no agents need apply. And a phone number. That's the picture I wanted."

Megan kicked the back of my seat hard enough to threaten whiplash. "I'm hungry," she whined.

"Me, too, kiddo." I put the car in gear and zipped up the windows.

"I know it doesn't look like much from here," Mom said. "But it's got a private walk across dunes, and the view is to die for. You like it, don't you, Megan?"

Great, now Mom was playing the grandchild card.

Day 2, Tuesday

To get my daily run in, I rose early enough that Mom and Megan would usually still be asleep when I returned. A thin smear of orange on the horizon predicted the sun would soon rise. Until I ran the first mile, an ocean breeze driving horsetail clouds up from the south chilled me. If I recalled my Boy Scout days correctly, those clouds meant we were likely to have rain in the next twenty-four hours.

Still several blocks from the beach, the crash of rollers put a smile on my face and got me thinking about the for-sale-by-owner condo Mom had discovered. Her parting words as we went to bed were, "Don't let someone buy it out from under you." With nearly four hours until the next high tide, I planned to run to the beach and take the hard-packed sand up to the condo. Running through the loose, dry sand was arguably better exercise, but not nearly as fun, and I was of an age that I wanted to enjoy my exercise.

I reached the beach moments before the top arch of the sun broke free of the sea, frosting the thin layer of clouds a neon pink. I stopped and watched the three-minute process of the sun wrenching itself from the sea's embrace and becoming a yellow orb floating free in the sky. A flock of black skimmers flew across the sun, and I cursed not having my camera to capture the brochure-worthy picture.

How could this not be a great day?

I continued my jog with renewed vigor and, if not for the For Sale sign, would have run past the condo. Seeing the ocean side of the building, I understood my mother's attraction to the place. Sliding glass doors and floor-to-ceiling windows ran the entire width of the first and second floors, confirming my impression that the floor plan was long and narrow. The first-floor doors led to a concrete patio. Placing the deck on the second floor allowed residents a view of the ocean unobstructed by the dunes. A third-floor dormer contained a sliding glass door leading to a recessed deck the width of the door.

I jogged up to the dune line for a closer look, my feet slipping and sliding in the dry sand. A tingle of anticipation ran down my spine. I verbalized the seven-digit phone number several times to embed it into my memory. The side units had good light, and with the three stories, I guessed the square footage at around twenty-five hundred—enough to allow Mom and me our own spaces, with plenty of room for Megan and her parents to escape Chicago for Christmas and Easter vacations.

From the deck, I could witness the play of rollers, count the number of waves between major crests, watch white foam surge up the beach, and listen to the hiss of the waves retreating to the sea in a series of streamlets. I could see myself rocking on the deck, watching the process repeat for hours on end, my personal serenity video.

A guy in a gray hoodie and black shorts sprinted

past on the hard-packed sand by the ocean, jerking me from my reverie. The stride, I decided, was too short to be the same person. Even so, it spoiled the idyllic mood I had constructed. Not everything on Tybee was perfect.

BECAUSE MY JOG HAD TAKEN extra time to scout the condo, my return found Megan and my mother dressed in jammies sitting on opposite sides of the dining room table. NPR news filled the air with commentary on the latest political nonsense from both parties. Mom was working on the crossword puzzle from the *New York Times*. A mug of steaming coffee sat on a coaster made from palm fronds a street vendor had thrust at us while we walked Savannah's River Street. Megan leaned over a pad of paper, mirroring my mother's habit of tapping her front teeth with the eraser end of a mechanical pencil while concentrating.

"Have you already done your daily crossword, Megan?" I walked to her and ruffled her coarse red hair, releasing the scent of her lemon shampoo. "Morning, Mom."

"She needs harder puzzles for her home-schooling," Mom said. "Finished hers in under five minutes."

"So whatcha working on, Pumpkin?" Megan had my artistic talents, which meant I had no idea what she was drawing.

"That man."

"Which man, Honey?"

"The man that stole Geema's phone."

I swallowed my correction of "that" to "who" and examined her drawing. She had made two lines from her stick figure representation to other parts of the paper. One led from a lower leg to what might be a circular spiderweb with a large bug in it. The other was a blow-up of the face. It depicted heavy eyebrows, cruel lips, and a goatee.

When had I learned to do cutouts like that? Surely not at six. "How come you're drawing this?"

She shrugged. "Just 'cause."

I kissed the top of her head. "You're doing a great job, kiddo. Much better than I could have ever done. After I shower, I'll make us oatmeal. Okay?"

She stopped tapping her teeth long enough to say okay.

I closed the door to my bedroom, called Detective Sergeant Issa, and was put right through. I described Megan's drawing. "She's the kind of kid who can become surprisingly obsessed if she's upset," I said in conclusion. "One of the genes I passed down. I'd like to head that off, but she has some good detail. If she could work with a police artist, we might kill two birds with one stone. She'd have the chance to work it out of her system, and given the detail she's drawing, you might end up with a decent picture of the thief."

"I'm sure Megan's a bright kid," Issa said. "But she's only six. Not exactly a reliable witness. Besides, we don't have the budget for sketch artists. Kill the old phone, get a new one, and let this go."

"How about if I paid for it?"

"I'm sorry, Mr. McCree. That's just not going to happen."

* * *

WHILE I WAITED FOR NINE o'clock to roll around—the time my mother thought acceptable for me to call the number listed for the condominium—I used a map app to determine its exact address. With that, my internet search confirmed the building held three units. The last time any of the units sold was before the 2008 housing crash. The middle unit had gone for $1,275,000. A search of the Chatham County tax records showed assessed values back into the 1990s. At its peak, the land for each unit had been valued at $600,000 and the improvements—the building itself—at $400,000, for a total of an even million dollars. Now the total assessed value was only $500,000.

I checked other nearby buildings. They also had experienced serious declines in their assessed values. From my earlier general research looking at other Tybee properties Mom had found "interesting," I was under the impression that housing prices had nearly regained 2008 levels. I guessed the owner would ask somewhere around $1.2 million, approximately the peak sales price less six percent because no sales agent was involved.

"It's nine," my mother called from Megan's bedroom, where the two of them were making the bed.

I turned off the radio and luxuriated in the blessed silence for a moment before dialing the number I had memorized. I introduced myself to the man who answered, and I said I wanted to know about the condo for sale by owner. "That was quick," he said.

"I only put the sign up yesterday afternoon. Oh, I should introduce myself. I'm the owner, Andy Beaufort."

I glanced at the tax record still on my computer screen. Owner was Andrew Russell Beaufort, which sounded like a southern name, but the guy's accent was decidedly northern. I had learned during my youthful stint on Wall Street as a bank stock analyst that I often received the best information from tight-lipped CFOs by using open-ended questions followed by silence on my part. Open-ended questions required something more than a yes or no answer, and most people felt a compelling need to fill silence and provided much more information than they might have intended. I started with my rehearsed question, "What can you tell me about the unit?"

He rattled on, giving its size (2,537 square feet), the association (two other great couples, I'd surely love them: nice, quiet people, hardly ever there), three full baths, three bedrooms, heat pump, central air, wood-burning stove. He petered out and I let the silence build.

"Only a one-car garage, but room for several more cars in the driveway as long as you're willing to jockey." After more silence on my part he added, "Are you looking to buy a place furnished or unfurnished?"

"I can go either way, depending on the value proposition. I take it you're leaving the area?" I mentally kicked myself at the yes-no question and promised myself to think before blurting the next question.

"Returning full-time to Rhode Island. What more can I tell you?"

"What are you asking?"

"It's good stuff, but seen a bit of wear and tear. I'd let it all go for the tax-deduction value, which I figure is roughly two thousand."

I chuckled both at his thinking and that he had given me the price of the furniture, but not the condo. "And for the condo?"

"I could screw around and wait for the right buyer and probably clear a million two after closing costs with a real estate agent, but I've got to start treatment for prostate cancer, and I really don't want to have to deal with negotiations and all that crap. I'd consider a million one fair."

It required effort on my part to tamp down my morbid curiosity about which treatment he was undertaking, whether it involved robotic surgery, and where he was being treated. He didn't need that from me. His urgency did give me negotiating leverage, however. With annoyance at myself for feeling guilty about taking advantage of his cancer, I rationalized that all real estate transactions are negotiations. After all, he might have dropped the bit concerning his cancer to elicit an empathetic reaction from me. "Sorry to hear about your cancer," I said to fill the silence my scatterbrain had created.

He'd indicated he was in something of a hurry. How much? "You offering financing?" I wasn't interested, but if he was receptive to carrying a loan, then he might be more receptive to bargaining if I paid cash. *Crud, another yes-no question.*

"Nah. Interest rates are still attractive. On the

other hand, I'd certainly be willing to knock a little off for a cash buyer if I could have this wrapped up before I go under the knife. What's your timing?"

"All I need to do is find the right place for the right price." I had no reason to tell him I had planned to buy with cash. Let him pay me for that. "When's a good time to take a tour? My mother will be coming along. The place is for her. And, you don't mind if I bring my granddaughter, do you?"

We agreed to meet at twelve-thirty. The timing would work well for me. My mother insisted that Megan had to wait at least an hour after lunch before she could go into the water—a rule she'd imposed on me during visits to the Massachusetts beaches while I was growing up. I found it absurd then and still did, but it wasn't worth fighting over.

"Oh, one last thing," I said before he hung up. I paused and formed an open question. "What can you tell me about renting your unit?"

"Owners do it all the time. I have the past few years' rental income available to share."

So much for the nice quiet couples who are hardly ever there. This was a guy who maybe didn't lie, but he didn't exactly fall over himself to tell the whole truth either. Of course, the same could be said of me.

IF IT HAD BEEN ONLY Megan and me, we would have walked to our appointment at the condo and caught lunch along the way. Even though it was less than a mile, Mom fretted about what we would do if we had an emergency later at the beach. "Mom," I said, "The emergency yesterday was caused by you not taking your phone on our walk, so I didn't know where you were and if you were okay. Just keep the new one turned on and everything will be fine."

Megan dawdled eating the triangles of peanut butter sandwich Mom made for lunch, something the child wouldn't have done if we had gone to a restaurant. Halfway through lunch, my daughter-in-law, Cindy, connected with my computer for a video call with Megan. Despite Cindy's attempts to steer the conversation to other things, all Megan could talk to her mother about was the man who had stolen Geema's phone.

I kept checking my watch until my mother said in exasperation, "She's your granddaughter. Make allowances. Call the guy and tell him we'll be fifteen minutes late."

So, grandchildren were closer to Godliness than promptness. I'd missed that lesson growing up. I called the owner, apologized, and told him we'd be thirty minutes late, which immediately dropped my angst. Of course, as soon as I said thirty, Megan hung up with her mother, ran to the bathroom, and appeared moments later wondering why we weren't ready to go.

I looked at my watch again, and this time Mom said, "If we're early, we're early."

I controlled the scope of Megan's dancing around by holding her two hands. Letting her pull against me, I said, "I heard you tell your Mommy that you didn't talk to the man who stole Geema's phone. You know I'm proud of you, because you don't talk with strangers. Right, Pumpkin?"

She stopped her gyrations and looked up with worry painted on her face. "Mommy and Daddy already told me that."

"Are you worried about the man who stole Geema's phone? You don't have to be, you know."

"Grampa Seamus will make sure he leaves you alone," Mom said.

Although he's already failed once.

"Give him a time out, Grampa Seamus."

"I'll keep it in mind."

We schlepped everything to the car and piled in, Megan providing us with a verbal transcript of her conversation with her mother. The kid had a memory, for sure, even if she didn't realize we had overheard the entire conversation.

We were on US-80 passing Sixth Street when Megan interrupted herself and yelled, "There he is."

At her shout, I automatically took my foot off the accelerator. I was already through the intersection before I interpreted that she had to be referring to the thief. She was pointing toward the beach. I knew that street dead-ended at the dunes with no intersecting streets. Not able to reverse because of the traffic, I accelerated, pulled in front of the car in the left lane, and cut through traffic to make a left and circle the block.

"Don't kill us, Seamus," Mother said through clenched teeth.

"Not my plan." I squealed around two more lefts, blasted through a yellow-maybe-orange light and back to the place where Megan had seen the guy.

We were the only thing moving on the street.

"Might be to the beach by now," Mom said.

I roared down the street looking for a parking spot. Finding none, I stopped in the middle of the street at the entrance to the boardwalk over the dunes onto the beach and hopped out. "Turn the car around, Mom."

I left the car door open, raced up the wooden boardwalk, and surveyed the beach. No sign of any guy who resembled the man we'd seen. I scanned the dunes themselves in case the guy had heard me coming and was hiding. All I spotted were two seagulls, heads tucked under their wings. No guys anywhere close to this boardwalk. Had Megan been seeing things, or had she seen him and he had entered one of the houses?

Should I knock on a few doors and see who answered? And if someone came to their door, I'd say what? It seemed like a good way to have a second interview with the Tybee Island police—one that would not go well for me. I did a 360 looking for anyone who resembled the man and gave it up. Megan had recently been talking to her mother and to me about the thief; maybe she had imagined the whole thing.

Mom had the car pointed up the street, so I slipped into the passenger seat. "I'm sorry, Pumpkin. I didn't see him."

"Good try, Grampa Seamus." Megan patted my head, echoing words and gestures I had often used when she tried something that didn't completely work out.

"Look on the bright side," my mother said, "now you won't be early for your appointment."

* * *

ANDY BEAUFORT MET US UNDER the awning at the condo's back door. Given his prostate cancer, I expected someone older. He looked fifty, although being tanned and fit with a full head of thick brown hair, he might not look his age. He was clean-shaven and carried with him a hint of aftershave lotion. He wore cordovan loafers, no socks, gray pants, and a Brooks Brothers polo shirt. A thin gold chain graced his neck. No finger jewelry. The guy exuded the good manners honed in a northeast boarding school.

Ushering us inside, he shook hands with us, including squatting down to Megan's level to exchange greetings with her. One of his knees popped as he rose, and my soccer knees ached in sympathy. "Football," he explained. "I'll get out of your way. If you have any questions, I'll be on the third-floor deck watching the cloud bank. It's amazing today."

Mom held Megan's hand while we explored. Behind the garage was a laundry room and behind that a media room with sliding glass doors to a covered patio where Andy stored a grill the size of my Prius. Carpeted stairs brought us to the main living floor. I couldn't imagine myself, let alone Megan, being disciplined enough to avoid tracking in sand and ruining that rug in short order. Mom and Megan led the way through the kitchen, bathrooms, and bedrooms. The furniture was good quality in an updated version of Danish Modern. It didn't show any of the wear I expected with rentals. Maybe I had misunderstood? In the living room my eye was captured by three large Klee prints from what I guessed were his late works.

The front opened onto a deck through another set of sliding glass doors. Floor-to-ceiling windows filled the wall and provided a wonderful view of the beach and ocean. The doors opened without difficulty, suggesting the building had not settled, and I stepped onto the deck, which was bathed in warm sunshine. A thousand yards beyond the beach, a cloud wall of the kind I associated with stories of Georges Bank boiled between the opaque sea and a luminous sky showing no hint of the rain forecast by yesterday's horsetail clouds.

Sparkling in the sun, the ethereal radar mast of a large ship floated above the misty rampart. In the water below, distant seagulls shimmered like stars in a night sky. I stuck my head back into the condo and called for Mom and Megan to come see. I pointed out the mast.

Megan said, "A pirate ship!"

During my explanation that the mast likely belonged to a cargo ship like those we had watched coming up and down the Savannah River the previous week, the fog bank rushed forward, hiding the mast from our view. It stopped its advance several yards from shore, retreated, before rolling onshore, blocking the sun and bathing us in the mist. The temperature dropped at least ten degrees, but before we became overly chilled, the fog retreated, once again revealing the sun.

"Again," Megan commanded while dancing in delight.

"You're lucky to have experienced that," Andy

called down from the deck above. "It doesn't happen often, but if your grandfather buys this place, you'll be able to see it again."

I laughed. "Unfair sales practices," I called back at him. "I'll be right up." I left Mom and Megan on the deck and wandered to the third floor, the master bedroom suite. The furniture was a different style featuring a cherry headboard, matching bureau and secretary with an open glass bookcase on top containing the only books I'd seen in the house. A mounted telescope stood in front of the fixed-door panel, and on the side table next to it was a well-thumbed *Sibley Guide to Birds*. In pride of place above the bed, I recognized a nicely matted and framed Robert Bateman print of a rough-legged hawk in an elm tree.

I joined him on the deck. "Good birdwatching from here?"

He shrugged a response. "Fog's about to leave. We'll soon see what it's hiding."

The fog dissipated and the container ship changed from phantom to a three-dimensional laser projection to a solid entity in air so clear I could read the hull registration numbers.

"What do you think?" he asked.

"Amazing sight."

"It is that, but I meant the condo."

"I'll have to see what Mom thinks. Megan's a fan, for sure. You mentioned you had rental information?"

He gestured me inside. "I got permission from one of the other owners to share his information since this place has never been rented out." He appeared embarrassed. "I don't like people using my things." He gave me another shrug. "Only child probably explains it."

He pulled a yellow folder from the desk cubbyhole and spread the papers on the table. The information from TBI Real Estate Management showed the middle unit had been fully rented May through October and one or two weeks a month during the off-season. Rental income would more than cover the maintenance, taxes, and insurance, including the huge cost for flood insurance.

"I made you a copy of the condo association agreement as well, plus copies of the electric bill. Anything else I can do to make this sale?"

"Lower the price." I laughed at his playful slap on my back.

"Come back with an offer and we'll talk. I'm motivated but not desperate."

Mom and Megan came upstairs, discussing which room would be Megan's and where she would store her beach toys. Beaufort excused himself and retreated to the kitchen.

They made a quick inspection of the third floor and agreed it would be Grampa Seamus's room. Megan began lobbying for beach time, and I ushered them downstairs to a waiting Beaufort.

"Based on their reactions," I said, "I'm also motivated, but not desperate either. I'll be in touch after I do a little due diligence."

"Sounds good. Just so you know, I have another buyer coming from work this afternoon. First reasonable bid gets my attention."

We hadn't more than closed the back door behind

us before Mom said, "This is perfect, Seamus. You need to get the man an offer."

"Mom, chances are that other buyer is somebody he made up to try to pressure us."

"I *love* it, Grampa Seamus," Megan said.

Were little girls born knowing how to twist their grandparents around their little fingers—or simply quick learners? "What did you like best, Pumpkin?"

"I can hear the ocean sing."

"And you wouldn't even have to leave the house to watch your birds," my mother chimed in. "Besides, you don't know for sure that the other buyer is made up."

"It's too far away for much birdwatching, Mom."

"Even so, you could walk onto the beach to watch your birds any time, and you could run on the beach without having to worry about traffic getting there, and Megan and I would both appreciate being able to come in from the beach and use our own bathroom instead of the stinky public ones. Right, Megan?"

"Right, Geema." They slapped hands, a high five for Megan and low five for my mother.

"And," my mother said, "it's got plenty of room for company. For the cost of a single bedroom condo in Boston with a thousand square feet and no view, you get twenty-five hundred square feet *on the ocean*."

"For Pete's sake, Mom. You're cherry picking the most expensive thing you found in the *Globe* real estate listings. I get the idea. You like it. I'll check it out."

Megan turned her baby blues up at me. "Are we moving tomorrow?"

* * *

THAT EVENING I DETERMINED THE condo met both our financial and spiritual objectives. Mom could live there mid-November through mid-April. I'd leave my place in Michigan's Upper Peninsula during mud season, which varied year-to-year but normally lasted three to four weeks sometime in March/April. If I decided staying all winter in the frozen woods at camp wasn't the good idea I thought it was right now, I could come down earlier. During the warmer months, I'd convert the place into a rental.

The rates Andy had shown me seemed reasonable compared to what we were paying for March at the place where we were staying. It wouldn't hurt to verify with an agency and learn how much they charged for arranging the rentals, cleaning between guests, changing linens, etc.

On a whim, I did an internet search on Andrew Russell Beaufort. It proved I was a bad judge of ages; he was in his late fifties. Only grandson of an old-line manufacturing company magnate, he had taken charge from his father, moved the factories from New England first to the South and then offshore. He sold the business to a Chinese conglomerate before the 2008 crash and spent his time mostly in seclusion on Martha's Vineyard managing his family charity. Never married. No known children.

The background made me wonder why he was selling. Probably didn't use it enough to justify the bother since he didn't like renting it out. My eyes kept pulling away from the condo information toward the corner of the table where Megan had continued to work on depicting "that man who stole Geema's phone."

Seeing a guy in a hoodie walking down Sixth Street had triggered her to again spend oodles of time drawing pictures of the man. Some had him standing over a little girl and her sand castle. Although the Tybee Island police weren't interested in having her work with a police artist, I wondered if it would help Megan put her worries to rest if I found someone who could bring out what she remembered—or thought she remembered.

During my years as a financial crimes consultant to various police forces, I had made acquaintances and friends with many police officers. Of those, Ashley Prescott of the FBI had the widest connections. It wasn't even nine p.m. her time, so I called. We caught up on her life and I explained the situation. Did she know anyone who could help Megan produce sketches of the man she'd seen?

"One name pops to mind," she said. "Kimberley Warren. She's retired. Writes crime novels, but I know she still freelances, especially working with abused kids, so she'd know how to work with Megan. You do know that no police department would use anything like a facial sketch that came from outside sources, especially if it involves a little kid?"

"My main concern is Megan. I'm afraid she picked up on everyone's worries about a strange man at the beach. It might help her, though. And who knows, if I show it to the police, it might trigger something for them."

"Kimberley's West Coast so you might yet catch

her tonight. Drop my name. I met her when we were both on the faculty at the Writers' Police Academy. We killed a bottle of wine trading stories of our undercover assignments. I'll text you her number once I look it up."

"Thank you. Thank you."

"Just don't hold it against me when you've wasted your money."

Within five minutes my phone buzzed and vibrated with a text alert. *I talked to Kim. She's expecting a call from a really nice guy. You can thank me later for the lie.* A second text message contained the phone number, which I dialed.

A voice, perhaps darkened by years of cigarette smoking, answered the phone. I confirmed it was Kimberley Warren and told her about Megan's continued concern about the guy we thought stole my mother's phone. "It's probably a phase she's going through, but still I think it would help her to have someone like you produce a sketch."

"Ashley sang your praises, Seamus, and asked me to give your request serious consideration. The good news is that I'm currently on the East Coast. My literary agent is retiring. I wanted to meet her replacement, and it gave me an excuse to spend a long weekend in New York. Long story short, the only window I have is tomorrow afternoon if I swing down to Savannah instead of heading straight home. That work?"

I had knocked on the door and it opened. I guessed I should walk through it. I sure hoped this was a good idea and not an expensive, harebrained Seamus scheme.

Day 3, Wednesday

THE HORSE-TAIL CLOUDS PREDICTING RAIN were premature by twenty-four hours. By the time I finished my Wednesday morning run, a light mist had become the steady rain forecasted to last all day. Megan and I shared her favorite breakfast cereal, Alpha-Bits, and worked on her school work together. Mom was right, Megan's parents needed to find her more challenging crosswords.

Mom and Megan taxied to the aquarium to give me space and time to understand renting realities and try to cut a deal on the condo Mom had her heart set upon.

I walked in unannounced at TBI Real Estate Management and told the receptionist I was considering buying a place on the ocean and needed to understand the rental business on Tybee.

With the squeak of a chair needing a shot of WD-40, she turned her back to me and pressed a button on her mini-switchboard. A phone buzzed in the rear, and the receptionist held a whispered conversation I could not hear. She faced me. "Miss Courtney will see you in a moment. If you'd like a seat?"

I preferred standing. Ninety seconds later, a big-haired platinum blonde with a thousand-watt smile arrived carrying a notebook computer tucked under one arm. "Mr. McCree? I'm Courtney Souchi, sales director." She held out her hand and we shook. "I understand you're looking to buy on Tybee and want to know how we can help you?"

She led me to a large conference room done up beach style: white table and chairs, beach umbrella artfully placed in a far corner, photos from around Tybee decorating the wall, and a coffee service contained in an old-fashioned wicker picnic basket. From somewhere I picked up that suntan lotion smell, or maybe it was my suggestive imagination. I refused any beverage, and we got down to business.

"I understand you already do some work for Mr. Andrew Beaufort?"

She entered his name into her notebook. "Be back in a jiffy." She brought back three yellow file folders. She opened one and perused its contents. "Oh yes, we monitor that home on a biweekly basis. We are the rental agent for the other two units in the building." She tapped the folders. "As a practical matter, I have whoever is cleaning those units check on Mr. Beaufort's at the same time. We also arrange monthly interior exterminating and twice-a-year exterior termite control. What services were you interested in discussing?"

"I don't want to mislead you, because I need to understand the economics of renting here before I sign a contract. So this may be a waste of your time."

She touched my arm with long fingers, each perfect nail a miniature beach scene. "Delighted to help." She gave me the dog and pony show, and I made notes of a few key figures. Beaufort had given me accurate rental information. "I need to be honest with you, Mr. McCree, it will be hit and miss this first year because many people have already booked. We don't recommend you lower your price just to assure occupancy. People often find a spot they like and will book year after year. But they're price sensitive. You need to tap the right sorts of people from the start."

Presumably the sorts who will pay big bucks. "So, I should assume no rent for the first year and be happy if some comes in?"

"It'll be better than that, but given the increase in flood insurance premiums Hurricane Matthew caused, the first year might be a money loser. After that it's normal."

I jotted a note to call a local insurance broker to get quotes. And I'd need legal counsel familiar with local real estate and title insurance practices. How did it work without brokers involved to prepare an offer sheet? Was there a generic contract I could download? I liked saving money, but also liked knowing professionals were vigilant on my behalf.

A light pressure of her fingernails on my arm brought me back to the room. "Anything else?"

"Maybe later. I do appreciate your time. Thank you."

"My pleasure, and be sure to tell Andy I said hi."

THE RAIN WAS MARGINALLY REDUCED as I walked the three blocks to where I had found a parking space, not realizing parking was free behind TBI's office. An itchy feeling crawled up the back of my neck. I spun around, expecting to see Courtney hurrying to tell me I had taken the wrong umbrella or something and caught the movement of someone stepping into a doorway. I waited but no one appeared or stuck their head around a corner. What was making me so nervous? Sure, I expected to make an offer on the most expensive property I had ever owned, but that shouldn't cause paranoia.

I reached my rental car without further incident and headed home—home being where I hung my hat, or in this case, my sopped raincoat. Shortly after turning onto US-80, I noticed a Toyota Land Cruiser behind me. It wasn't close; it wasn't far, but it again made me hair-tingling-the-back-of-my-neck nervous. *Get a grip, Seamus.* Who would trail me with a monster vehicle that couldn't hide behind a Mack truck? First, somebody *didn't* follow you while you were walking. Now, someone *isn't* following you while you drive down the main street in town.

Still, a wise woman who was a bodyguard once told me to always assume you are being followed so the one time that you are, you recognize it. Nerves on edge, I drove past my normal turn and instead chose a street I knew would dead end. I flicked on my blinker and executed the maneuver. The Land Cruiser had room to go around me, but it too slowed. No blinker for them. Between light glare and tinted windows, I couldn't see the driver.

I crept down the street pretending to look for a parking space. Using my side mirror, I monitored the black Land Cruiser's progress. It moved slowly through the intersection. The driver glanced in my direction.

He wore a hoodie.

I did a three-point turn, which was good for me. I usually require at least seventeen points on a narrow street. By the time I reached the intersection, the Land Cruiser had vanished. I hadn't hallucinated since college, when I unknowingly ate the wrong kind of fungi in a mushroom and avocado sandwich at a friend's house.

Maybe Megan's over-concern about the guy who stole my mother's cell phone was making me a touch paranoid. Freud reportedly said "sometimes a cigar is just a cigar." And, I reminded myself, sometimes a hoodie is just apparel.

BACK AT THE RENTED HOUSE, I was running on borrowed time before Megan and Mom would return from the aquarium. I lined up an insurance broker to provide estimates of condo and FEMA flood insurance and a real estate lawyer, who would review contracts and take care of the title search and insurance. He sent me a template to submit my proposal to Beaufort. I completed the parts that wouldn't change and left three critical areas blank: offer price, date of possession, and whether the deal was contingent on obtaining a mortgage, which I hoped to use as a small bargaining chip.

My stomach growled, protesting a long-delayed lunch. I wolfed down a couple of Mom's yogurts, which tasted like chalk but did dampen my hunger pains. Still no sign of Mom and Megan, although they needed to get back within the hour because the police sketch artist would arrive around two-thirty. I inhaled deeply, felt the weight settle into my lungs, and held it for a slow release—it wasn't every day I committed myself to seven-figure investments—and dialed Beaufort. It bounced immediately to voice mail. While he droned on about leaving a message, I wondered whether I was better off waiting a minute or two and dialing again or leaving a message. His message beeped and like Pavlov's dog I spoke, "This is Seamus McCree. I'd like to make a proposal to buy your condo but have a couple of questions first. Please give me a call."

The thunder of Megan's footsteps up the stairs announced her return. Mom followed and dropped her fanny pack on a chair, mumbled she was exhausted and planned a three-day nap. Megan launched a nonstop recital of exactly what they had seen in which tank.

Her recital exhausted me, and all I had to do was listen. Some men think it's great to become a father in their late fifties or sixties, or some extreme fools in their seventies. Spending two weeks with Megan made me glad my only child, Paddy, had completed college before I was fifty.

Megan was relating a long, convoluted story involving endangered sea turtles when the doorbell rang. Had to be the police sketch artist.

* * *

KIMBERLEY WARREN STOOD ON THE stoop holding a newspaper over her head with one hand; the other held a large portfolio case. She was only a couple inches shorter than my six two, tucked her shoulder-length hair behind her ears, wore no makeup that I could see, which probably meant she was expert at applying it. Rain drops spotted her pressed blouse. Cropped pants stopped a half dozen inches above running shoes that meant business. Her sneakers squeaked in the vestibule. She removed them and her running socks.

"Are your feet cold?" I asked. "I can give you some clean, warm socks." I blushed, realizing that what I had intended as a hospitable gesture might be interpreted as presuming more intimacy than warranted, and rushed on, "Thanks so much for doing this. Megan's upstairs. She doesn't know you're coming. I didn't want her worrying all day."

"Good idea." She motioned us upstairs. "In fact, let's not tell her exactly what I'm doing. I'll fill her in. I'd like you to sit somewhere to the side so she knows you're around, but not directly in her line-of-sight."

I introduced her to Megan as Ms. Warren.

"If it's okay with your grandfather," she said. "I'd prefer you called me Kim. And can I call you Megan, or would you prefer Ms. McCree?"

That got Megan giggling and the two began talking as if they'd been best friends for all of Megan's six years. Kim eased a sketch pad onto the table and doodled while they talked. I wanted to watch her work, but those were not my marching orders, and I wasn't going to screw it up. She was the pro; I let her do her work.

"I understand your great-grandmother was robbed," Kim said.

"Your Geema," I said.

Megan's smile vanished. Her shoulders slumped. I wanted to give her a hug and tell her it was okay. I must have sent off vibrations because Kim shot me a warning look.

"He got very close to you," Kim said, "didn't he?"

Megan cautiously nodded.

"Did he scare you?"

Megan shook her head, and I wanted to tell her to "use her words," but I stifled the impulse.

"What were you doing when he came near you?"

"Making a castle for ocean fairies."

"That's important work . . . and hard, too. Did he say anything to you?"

Headshake.

"Or touch you. Maybe pat your head or put his hand on your shoulder?"

Headshake.

"Can you tell me what he did do, Megan?"

"Made a shadow. I took a picture."

"You took a picture of him?"

Megan held her hands to the side of her eyes and brought the middle fingers of each hand down to meet her thumb. She blinked her eyes and jerked the middle fingers away from her thumbs, making a clicking sound with her tongue—taking a picture with her eyes.

"She has a strong eidetic memory," I said. Seeing confusion play on Kim's face, I added, "Photographic memory. Kids can be really good at it, but most start losing their abilities around Megan's age. We don't make a big deal of it, but it's strong in her—not just a proud Grampa Seamus talking. She often does best with specific questions."

Kim drew Megan's attention by lightly touching her hand. "Would you like to tell me what this man looked like? For example, could you describe his hair?"

"Brown."

"Long like mine or short like your Grampa Seamus."

They discussed hair (widow's peak, although Megan didn't know the term) and eyes (darker brown than his hair) and ears (couldn't tell because of the hoodie) and nose (fat and not crooked like Grampa Seamus), no smile, no dimples in cheeks, no facial hair other than the goatee. All the while Kim continued sketching, never showing Megan what she was doing.

Megan interrupted the proceedings to use the bathroom. I brought Kim sweetened tea and Megan lemonade. Kim worked forty-five minutes before she rotated her pad and asked Megan if her sketch looked like the man.

Megan hesitated. "A little."

"Point to what doesn't look right," Kim said.

Megan immediately pointed to the eyes and under Kim's questioning indicated they were too close together and the eyebrows should be bushier. They continued working, making incremental improvements until Megan showed signs of frustration.

"What's the matter, Pumpkin?"

"It's not right. I feel bad."

"You're frustrated because it's not perfect, and you can't explain to Kim what needs to change?"

Megan nodded. Tears leaked down her cheeks.

"Aw, Honey." Kim gave Megan a hug and wiped the tears with her fingers. She wiggled Megan around until they were both giggling. "You've done great. Much better than the adults I work with. Do you think I would recognize this guy if I met him on the beach?"

Megan shrugged in answer.

"Did you tell Kim about his tattoo?" I prompted.

Megan raced to her room and returned to present Kim with her sketchbook. Kim oohed and aahed at Megan's drawings. "Computer with internet access?" she asked over her shoulder.

I fetched my laptop and with Megan curled in her lap, Kim searched for spider web tattoos. "Tell me if any of these look close to the one he had."

Megan took control of the laptop and finger-swept her way through images with one hand while sucking the other thumb. My grandkid needed a nap. She kept flipping through images until she found one she was moderately satisfied with. I bookmarked the circular web with an oblong spider for future reference.

"Time for me to chauffer you to the airport," I said. "There's a place along the way I can have copies made of the sketch. Megan, let's have Geema read you a story."

I conspired with my mother to get Megan comfy so she could fall asleep without admitting she needed a nap. Once Kim and I were in my car and on our way to the mainland, Kim said, "This was great fun.

What a delightful granddaughter you have. I almost feel guilty for charging you."

"I can think of ways to assuage your guilt." Heat flushed my face. "I didn't mean that as a come-on. I meant a reduced fee or something."

She belted out a deep chest laugh. "*Almost*, Seamus, *Almost*. What's next?"

I considered the question before answering. "First thing, I hope Megan can now put the incident behind her. As you could see from her notepad, she's been fretting. On the way home, I'll show the local constabulary the spider web tattoo and your sketch and watch them like a hawk to see if it rings any bells."

"Do you know anyone in a big, black, SUV?"

My stomach knotted with a dull pain.

"It's been behind us since we hit the main drag. Two cars passed you when you slowed way down while thinking how to answer my question. This guy matched your speed and let another car pass him. He's one car back."

Ahead was the entrance for Fort Pulaski. I grabbed my phone and pressed the icon for camera mode. Without signaling, I pulled into the turnoff, jerked open the car door, and snapped pictures of the front and rear of a Toyota Land Cruiser as it roared past.

"Subtlety," Kim said, "is not your forte."

BY THE TIME I SAW Kim off at the airport and returned to Tybee Island, it was nearly five o'clock. The police station was on my way, and figuring it was harder to ignore someone in person than it was to ignore a phone call, I dropped in unannounced to see if I could catch Detective Sergeant Brittney Issa.

She made me wait just three minutes before she escorted me into a room and sat us at a long table by the only spot not covered with piles of paper. "You're beginning to feel like a bad penny, Mr. McCree. Now what?"

I slid her a copy of Kim's sketch. "This guy look at all familiar to you?" I had to explain what I had done. She gave me a look that suggested I needed a mental exam.

"I'll show it around to the department since you went to the trouble. Haven't been any more reports of stolen phones, so maybe whoever it was has moved on."

"I think he's been busy following me." I brought up the cell phone picture I had taken of the rear of the black Toyota Land Cruiser that Kim believed was following us. "Here's the plate. Why not run it through your system and see what comes up?"

"Are you one of those cop wannabees? A modern-day Batman?"

I'd heard this refrain before from police officers feeling threatened when their departments had called in my services to "help" them with one of their cases. In my next life, maybe I'll learn to take their small-minded perspective in stride. I counted to ten before I spoke using precise diction to try to control my anger. "If I had wanted to be a cop, I could have been one in Boston, where my father was a sergeant and killed on duty. Feel free to check me out. I'm the only Seamus McCree in the U.S. It should be easy for a real detective." I tapped the copy of the sketch. "I did this to help my granddaughter stop worrying, and I shared it with you because I thought you might find it useful. That Land Cruiser followed me at least twice. The sketch artist, a thirty-year veteran from L.A., was the one who spotted the tail."

I pushed the chair back so hard it toppled to the floor with a bang. "So if you think I'm Loony Tunes and lying through my teeth, that's on you. I'm clear about what I've done. Have a good fucking day, Detective Sergeant Issa."

"Wait," she called after me. "Wait!"

She had my local address and phone number. She could damn well contact me if she wanted to continue this conversation.

A NOTE FROM MOM ON the kitchen table informed me that Megan had left a message on my cell phone to tell me the two of them were eating dinner at Huc-a-Poos in case I wanted to join them. With no indication of what time they'd left, I figured I'd call and determine if I still had time to meet them. I searched my backpack for my phone. Not there.

I patted down pockets without success and figured I had left it in the car. Halfway down the back stairs to the driveway, I froze at the click of the house door automatically locking. *Oh crap.* In my hand was the key fob for the car. Again, self-pat-down produced nothing. I could visualize the house keys sitting on the kitchen table, right where I had laid them.

I had locked myself out. Worse, I discovered the cell phone wasn't in the car.

Leaning against the still warm car hood, I retraced my path to meeting Detective Issa. I'd shown her the photos using the phone before I got my dander up and stormed from the conference room. I must have left it. *What a Stoopid Mick I am.*

If I walked to Huc-a-Poos, I might miss Mom and Megan. I could twiddle my thumbs and wait for Mom to let me in. Either way, I'd have to fess up to leaving the phone at the station. If I owned up to the reason I left it, Mom would rib me about my temper for the next millennium or two. I could drive to the police station and pick up the phone, but my wallet with my license was in the backpack in the house. Given my departure from Issa was not on the best terms, I could expect no mercy from the police if I got in an accident or pulled over. *More paranoid thinking.* Although the SUV following me had been real.

Had the owner left a spare key in one of those fake rocks or under a loose garden brick? Checking proved fruitless, leaving me two choices: wait outside for my mother or walk to the darned station, take my licks from Issa, walk back, and only fess up to locking myself out of the house. Maybe a walk would help clear my head.

While still dithering, a red sports car pulled into the driveway. It took me a moment to realize the driver was a tank-top, short shorts, sandal-wearing, red-toenail painted version of Detective Issa. She slid out holding up my phone. Her police uniform had hidden a very attractive woman.

"I believe this is yours." She wore a big "gotcha" smile.

"I just realized where I left it. It sure diminishes the intended effect of storming out of your office, doesn't it?" I accepted the proffered phone. "You could have called."

"And what, listen to the phone ring in my hand? Besides, I wanted to continue our discussion. Invite me in?" She leaned into the car and retrieved a satchel-style purse.

How to finesse this? "We can talk here."

"Did you lock yourself out of the house?"

She didn't make Detective Sergeant just because she looked good. "Yep. Sure did. Two for two on the stupid front and the day's not done. My mother would say it was karma for losing my temper."

"Speaking of your family, where are they?"

I told her the whole story of how I came to lock myself outside.

"News flash. You're human. You're permitted to laugh at yourself. If I get you inside, can we start over from the beginning?"

"You know where a spare key is? I couldn't find one."

"Nope, but I'm excellent at picking locks. And unlike the open book I discovered about you on the internet, you won't find that secret anywhere online. Which means, if I let you in, I'll know it's you if I see it on Facebook or whatever." She raised her eyebrows and her smile warmed.

She'd researched me? Well, I had challenged her. "Fair enough. If you're off-duty," I indicated her casual clothes, "I have wine and beer."

"Either white wine or dark beer would do nicely. I'm officially in civilian mode to avoid running up

OT, but I'd like to discuss that license plate picture you snapped."

Mom had a bottle of chardonnay I'd happily donate to the cause of learning why Issa was here. "Open white chilling in the fridge okay?"

"To be clear, you are authorizing me to enter this house, which you are renting."

I agreed and walked her to the door. Previously, I had treated her the way I treated any police sergeant; but now, as she examined the lock, I had an interesting view of her heart-shaped rear. I must have been observing too carefully because without looking away from her task, she said, "Like the view?"

I proved I could still blush. "Very much, thanks. How's the lock going?"

"We're in." She walked in ahead of me. Her athletic legs easily mastered the stairs, and her rear glided nicely from side-to-side.

I suspected her sashay was for my benefit, and I appreciated the show. She spotted the powder room and ducked in. Through the closing door she said, "Apologies. I left in a hurry."

Pouring her a chardonnay and myself a glass of red, I arranged Triscuits around the outside of a dinner plate and sliced and stacked cheddar and pepper-jack cheese artistically in the middle—well, as artistically as I ever could, which meant I created two half circles of overlapping pieces. *Good Housekeeping* was unlikely to be coming to me for entertaining tips.

I placed the wine glasses and crackers and cheese on the coffee table and, feeling at a loss, picked up my wine glasses and remained standing. She could choose her seat; it wasn't like this house had a view or anything that I'd reserve for a guest.

She returned from the bathroom, and I handed her the wine glass and with a wave indicated she could sit wherever she wanted.

"Couch's good." She pulled a tablet from the purse she placed between her feet. "I have something to show you."

She plopped down on the middle cushion of the three-cushion sofa. She'd picked the lock left-handed, so I chose her right side to avoid clunking wine glasses. She finger-swiped the tablet alive to an article on the Savannah daily newspaper's website. "Read." She handed me the tablet and sipped her wine. "Good choice." She collected two Triscuits and covered one with a slice of cheddar and one with the pepper-jack. Ate one, took a healthy sip of wine, and ate the second cracker. "Reading means you turn your attention from me to the tablet."

Again, my face warmed with a blush. I skimmed the article. A car-theft operation had been busted the week before in Savannah. At the time of the raid, they confiscated four high-end cars: two Beamers, one Lexus SUV, one Porsche. Two mechanics were under arrest. The investigation was continuing according to a police spokesperson.

She handed me a loaded Triscuit. "The license plate image you captured belongs to the Lexus. The guys they caught seem to be fully cooperating. Their job was to give the cars a thorough mechanical inspection to make sure they're in top condition, change the oil, top fluids, and put on fresh tires if the tread showed significant wear. Their records show they ran an average of ten cars a week through the place. That's five hundred a year given they received two weeks of paid vacation around Christmas."

"Paid vacation?" My voice rose in my incredulity.

"They've worked there two and three years. They both claim to have no idea what happens to the cars after they do their thing."

"So not a chop shop. Throwing them into containers and shipping them overseas for sale?"

She stopped her wine glass halfway to her mouth, gave me what I assumed was an approving side glance, and finished her sip. "The guys say that when they're done with the cars, they park them in the lot, and the next morning the cars are gone."

"And they never thought that was peculiar?"

"They each cleared a hundred grand a year, plus 401(k), medical, dental, and life insurance, and the previously mentioned two-weeks' vacation. Plus, they ran a legitimate repair shop with a great online rating."

"They were paid on the books?" I drank some of the red. "That's novel. With those benefits, there must be an owner of record."

"My source says the corporate legal spaghetti dead-ends in the Cayman Islands. Just your cup of tea. What made you conclude they were shipping them overseas?"

"They can't be stealing five hundred high-end cars a year in Savannah. It's got to be a wide-ranging theft ring that brings them to Savannah because it's the second largest port on the East Coast. Ship them abroad and get a lot more value than recycling them here." A glance assured me she had followed my logic—or already knew it and was testing me. "So, the two in custody have never seen who picks up the cars?"

"They don't know who leaves them either. The cars are there in the morning with keys left in the drop box."

I drained my glass and leaned back into the cushions, linked my fingers behind my head, and closed my eyes. What the hell did this mean? The plates from a stolen Lexus SUV were riding on the Land Cruiser that Kim and I were sure had followed me. Why would a guy involved in an auto theft ring follow me? And how did a car ring relate to my mother's stolen phone? Were they using stolen phones to contact one another? Seemed damned risky for an outfit that had to be netting millions a year and could surely afford inexpensive, legal burner phones. "How did you connect the dots?"

"After your dramatic departure and challenge to look you up, I did. Seamus Anselm McCree. Wall Street golden boy dramatically quits and begins helping police departments solve financial crimes and a few murders along the way. The articles didn't mention your good looks, which I noticed all on my own. Anyway, with your bona fides established, I did what you asked and ran the plate from your photo. Discovering it belonged to a different car than the one it was on got me remembering the article." She pointed to the tablet. "I called the Savannah folks in charge of the investigation and got a bunch of intel on their operation."

"Wow, I thought you needed to pull teeth to get another department to give up information on an ongoing case."

"Usually true, but this is one of those small-world things. It just so happens one Lieutenant Issa is heading the investigation. All the Issas in Chatham County are related, and this one is my ex, who still has misplaced hopes that we'll get back together. So when I tell him what I've got, he gives me the inside dirt. I no sooner hang up than one of my officers brings in your cell phone, and here I am with an empty glass of wine and no one waiting for me at home."

Really. I took our glasses and the nearly empty cracker plate to the kitchen and refilled everything. I felt certain there was more to this story, but I had no idea where it might lead. It was a good time to remind myself that my first impression of Sergeant Issa was of a woman who was good at catching ants with honey.

She watched me return, balancing the plate while carrying both filled wine glasses. "A man of many talents."

I let her comment go without response, handed back her wineglass, and settled onto the couch.

She laid a hand lightly on my forearm. "Seamus, I'm concerned about what you might have gotten yourself into."

That she had used my first name and had not removed her hand from my arm distracted me from the meaning of her words until they finally sank in. "What else aren't you telling me? It sounds to me like the guy who stole Mom's cellphone might be the guy who takes delivery of the stolen cars. The car he's driving either went through the shop shortly before Savannah busted them or—wait a minute. For a bust like that, they must have been watching the shop for a while, right? They should have seen the cars delivered and later removed. Followed the ones leaving the shop. Shouldn't they already know everyone involved—at least the little guys, not necessarily the kingpins?"

"They did nail the two people they observed delivering cars. Thing is, they never saw the cars leave."

"You're kidding? How could they—?"

"Long story short, building records indicated a lower level. A building inspector uncovered the hidden controls to a lift down to that floor, which was much larger than on the building plans. It had room for a hundred cars plus an underground passage to another building nearly a quarter mile away in the same industrial park. The other building is owned by another corporation my ex says is part of the same interlocking corporate structure."

"Consistent. What did they learn from the delivery guys?"

"They're college kids making some scratch on the side. They get a text message with a time and location. They find an unlocked car with two hundred bucks and a new burner phone on which they receive the next text. They each were asked by some nice woman they only saw the once and described so vaguely we have no clue what she looks like."

I noticed she hadn't had any more of her wine, but I used sipping mine to give me time to sort it out. Two sips later I admitted the whole situation made no sense to me. "What's concerning you that I'm too dense to see?"

She leaned back, putting both hands behind her head, squinched one eye shut, and gazed at the ceiling with her other eye. Facing me, she said, "Here's a scenario. Tell me what you think. The car ring gets hit and someone involved learns you're in town."

"How could they learn that?"

"You said yourself you're the only Seamus McCree in the country. Is it a coincidence that one of the foremost experts on financial crime happens to show up? They're not sure, and they tell the guy in the hoodie—one of their drivers, maybe—to follow you. Hoodie sees an opportunity to steal what he thinks is your phone and gets your mother's instead."

"To see who I've been talking to?"

"Or see where you've been if you used your GPS. Who knows? Point is, megabucks are involved here, and you and your family fell smack into it when you came here for your vacation."

"That is so far-fetched. It's impos—"

"Fine. You give me a scenario that explains everything." She covered up that same "gotcha" smile I had seen before by drinking her wine.

I finished mine in a gulp and admitted to having no alternative explanation. "So, if we go with your scenario, what's your recommendation?"

"I will deny saying this, since it's not exactly good for business in a tourist town. Take your family and leave."

I gaped at her in disbelief. Why the hell would I do that? The Irish stubbornness in me rose quickly to the surface. I'd be gin swiggered if I'd turn tail and run. "Your force is looking out for the Land Cruiser?"

"Sure. But do you really think the guy will keep those wheels when he knows you made them? Next time it'll be a soccer mom's minivan or a plain-Jane sedan. The loss of their facilities is a blow, but nothing compared to what they'd lose if someone—someone like you—brought down their financial empire. Assume they consider you a threat. We are not far from Savannah, where they whack a guy at least once a week. A short drive to Tybee, take care of all three of you, mix in with the beach crowds, and three more unsolved. You're just statistics and fading memories."

Even if this crazy scenario were true, I knew Mom wouldn't back away from this—she's the one who raised me. But Mr. Hoodie knew exactly what Megan looked like, and in following us he probably knew where we were staying, maybe even where Mom and Megan were dining out. I considered calling my mother and thought better of it. No reason to panic them. No reason to panic at all. It was a far-fetched possibility, but one we needed to discuss with both Megan's parents and my mother. Did Issa have more she wanted to tell me? "I'm looking at buying a condo here, so what's Plan B, assuming we don't scare away?"

"I'm going to give you my direct number." She handed me my phone from the table. "Put it on speed dial under Brittney."

"What'll that do?"

"Can't ask a girl for a date if you don't know how to get ahold of her, now can you?"

I added the number under Issa, Brittney (Tybee Sgt.)

She rose and I followed suit. "Look, I only get to meet three kinds of guys. I've already learned that cops in a relationship is a bad idea. I apologize for thinking you were a wannabe, but I see a lot of them. And then there're the guys who don't want to deal with a woman cop. Too threatening to their manhood. You stood up to me and I respect that. I've seen how you deal with your granddaughter. If you're planning to be around, I'd like to know you better." She looped her arm through mine. "Be a gentleman and show me out."

Nothing about her appearance was objectionable. I'd had relationships with cops before, but something here did not add up. Escorting her downstairs, I mulled over various ideas. Was it possible she was part of the car theft ring and that's how she had learned so much about the operation? That seemed even more unlikely than me being a target of the ring because I was a financial crimes expert.

At the bottom of the stairs, I went to disengage so I could open the door. She pinned my elbow to her side, slid her other arm around me. "I could stand a goodnight kiss," she said.

I leaned in to give her a peck and her lips were on mine, hard. Her body pressed against me from chest to thighs, and she moaned softly.

It had been too long since I had kissed a woman. My body reacted even though my mind was sending alarm bells. I opened my mouth and our tongues commenced a slow tango. My hands slipped down to her firm glutes. Our tongue dance quickened, and she ground into my hardness.

From outside came the crunch of tires on the

gravel driveway. My pounding heart kicked up a notch as I recalled her warning words. Was this the attack she had predicted? I broke our clutch and ducked an eye to the spy-hole in the door. Megan danced circles beside a taxi while Mom extracted her car seat. "They're back."

Issa laughed. "Timing is everything." She fluffed her tank top. "Well, now I need a cold shower."

I finger-combed my hair and hoped the bulge in my pants wasn't obvious.

Issa stepped past the threshold and faced me. "Let me know." She formed her lips into a silent kiss and winked before greeting Megan and my mother, chitchatting about what kind of pizza they had and thanking Megan for her part in creating the sketch.

Megan raced past me into the house.

"What was that about?" Mom waited at the top of the stairs watching me carry the car seat into the house.

"Complications," I said.

"Where there's a woman and you, there are always complications. You're red as a beet."

Day 4, Thursday

Andy Beaufort left a message while I was on my morning run. He'd been out of town all day yesterday and could meet anytime today to discuss a purchase. No reason to wait to call until Mother's polite nine o'clock for a guy who'd phoned me already this morning. Once we agreed to meet at his condo around nine-thirty, I asked, "What do you want for a deposit?"

"My lawyer has an escrow account. I know deposits are often up to ten percent, but I don't think you're out to screw me, so would ten grand be okay?"

"Sure. What's the lawyer's name?"

"It's Bill Przybylski. I'll call and get the formal name of the escrow account or whatever. I've never done this before."

I had him confirm the spelling. The conversation fizzled after he hinted that we could negotiate by phone, and I ignored the suggestion. I wanted to see his reactions to my bid, not make a blind deal.

My next call was to my son, Paddy. He and his wife had video conferenced with Megan daily, so he knew about Mom's stolen phone and Megan's sketch. The evening before, I had completed the picture for them by describing my meeting with Detective Sergeant Brittney Issa—well, the more-or-less official part of that encounter. Paddy wanted to discuss the situation with his wife before deciding whether to send Megan home.

"We don't want Megan to be fearful about working with the police. We run some risk all the time with the Chicago crime gangs." He didn't need to explain that. I figured it was nerves talking. I had met Cindy during her stint as a cub investigative reporter in Chillicothe, Ohio, where she'd helped me solve a series of crimes. As the senior investigative reporter for a Chicago TV station, she now antagonized not only the crime gangs, but crooked politicians. I refocused on what Paddy was saying. ". . . and we're not running away. But if anything happens to increase the risks, let's get her on a plane home."

I agreed with the plan, and he shifted gears and asked about the place I was hoping to buy. I gave him the address so he could look online. "We'll see how the negotiations go later today."

"Fingers crossed. Give Megan a kiss from Cindy and me."

I planted a loud smack on Megan's head and decided to walk to Beaufort's condo. While I had been plenty warm while running, I was one layer short of being comfortable. The day was to warm up nicely, so I increased my pace rather than return for a jacket. That ended up a good decision because I arrived, with no spotted tails, a hair before the appointed time. Beaufort served fresh-squeezed orange juice on the deck warmed by an outdoor heater. Negotiating proved easier and quicker than I expected. I told him I'd pay cash and could complete the transaction within a week provided the inspection and title search were okay. We agreed on a million even. The big stuff concluded, I asked. "Have you decided how much you want for your furnishings?"

"To be honest, I don't want to have to move the stuff. Say twenty-five hundred for everything that's here?"

"By everything you mean . . .?"

He waved his hands in an inclusive manner. "Anything that's here. I give you the key, you move in. If there's something you don't want, it's your responsibility to get rid of it. Fair enough?"

More than fair. The furniture was used but of good quality. I knew his Bateman framed print was worth a grand by itself. If those were Klee prints? And what about the Zeiss scope I'd seen in the third-floor bedroom? "You don't mean everything, do you? Not the scope in your bedroom?"

Confusion painted his face before it cleared up. "No, it slipped my mind. And my offer doesn't include the Mercedes in the garage either." He laughed. "And I'll remember to take my photographic gear, too. And I'll clean out the fridge! You get my drift, though? Twenty-five hundred. Personal check at closing will be fine."

We shook and signed the contract I had brought. I left feeling I might have gotten a better deal if I had negotiated harder, but it had already seemed too easy.

On the walk home, I called my lawyer and asked him to complete the title search and line up title insurance on a priority basis. He thought he'd be able to have the inspector check the house either late that day or tomorrow. I confirmed with the insurance agent that it was a go; I'd give him the policy start date once we agreed on the closing date.

This deal was falling into place nicely, except for my sense of unease that would not go away. I thought again of the Bateman, the Klee-like prints downstairs, and my sense that Andy Beaufort had forgotten he had a telescope worth a couple Gs in the upstairs bedroom. Maybe the guy was distracted with his upcoming prostate surgery. I'd been lucky and not had any major health issues, so I couldn't say how focused I'd be if I were facing his situation. I should cut the guy a break.

Megan greeted me at the door with a request to run through her addition flash cards. In a negotiating mood, I countered with, "Only if we do subtraction, too." She quickly agreed. Our addition game was to see how long she needed to go through the complete deck up to twelve plus twelve. Any errors added ten seconds. She was practicing to beat her mother. She had arrived last week having trouble only with sums involving eight. She was now answering those correctly and picking up speed daily. Her mother would be in for a surprise the next time she played math facts with Megan.

Subtraction was her greater challenge. I had removed the elevens and twelves from the deck so she could work with her fingers on any that stumped her. Despite Megan's wanting to be timed, I was concentrating with her on accuracy.

Halfway through the subtraction exercise, she answered seven minus five correctly and asked. "What's five minus seven?"

Growing up, I constantly pestered my mother

with why and how questions. She had never once told me I had to wait until I was older before she'd answer. I had taken the same approach with Paddy. Mom said from the other room, "I can't wait to hear this one."

"Bring seven blocks, Megan."

Mom came in and perched on the couch arm. Megan brought seven green wooden rectangular solids from her room and dropped them with little thumps as they hit the carpeted floor. I had her line them up in front of us with all seven blocks on her side of a pencil I placed between us. "Okay, if you have seven blocks, and you give me five, how many blocks do you have left?"

"Two." She gave me five blocks and kept two for herself.

"For now," I said. "Give your two blocks to Geema." Once she did, I continued. "Now to your question: how many blocks do I have left if I start with five and give you seven?"

She shook her finger at me. "You can't. You don't have seven."

"Okay, so let's work this out. I need to give you seven." Counting, I handed her five blocks one at a time. "How many more do I need to give you?"

She wrinkled her brow in concentration, then her frown lifted. "Two?"

"Exactly, Pumpkin. I owed you seven, but I only gave you five, so I still need to give you two more. But I don't have two more, do I? To give you two more, I'm going to have to get them from somewhere else. Where can I find two blocks?" I looked at my mother to give Megan a hint.

"Geema." She clapped her hands in delight.

"Will you give them to me, Mom?"

"Nope," my mother said. "But, I'll lend them to you."

"Megan," I said, "what does it mean if Geema lends me something?"

Megan formed her lips into a pout and shook her head.

"It means I have to give them back to her. It means she'll let me have them, but I promise to pay her back for them. So, if I take the two from Geema." Mom handed me the two blocks. "And give them to you, have I given you seven blocks?"

She looked at the seven blocks in front of her. I could see her mentally count them. She nodded affirmation.

"So, I started with five. I gave you seven, but I owe Geema two. That's the answer. I owe Geema the difference between seven and five. Do you see?"

Megan shook her head. "You can't give them to me. They're not yours. Here, Geema." Megan handed my mother the two blocks I had borrowed. "You cheated, Grampa Seamus. Papa gave me a time out when I gave away a toy that wasn't mine."

"Right you are, Pumpkin. I am so screwed."

"Seamus," Mom said. "Language."

"Mom, will you finish the flashcards with Megan and have her read to you for a while? I have some things I need to do on the computer."

A dull ache pulsed behind my eyes. Why hadn't I thought to do this earlier? I did an image search on the computer for Andrew Russell Beaufort. It wasn't a unique name, and the guy was a semi-recluse. With a few search modifications, I found the one who lived in Rhode Island. The society pages of the *Boston Globe* contained a picture of Beaufort attending a gala at the Symphony four years ago. He was bald, had a thin, hooked nose, and looked his age.

The only way the Andy Beaufort I had just paid ten grand to was the guy in this picture was if he wore a wig and had undergone a nose job to make his massive.

Or the *Globe* had mislabeled the picture.

That faint hope died minutes later. I found multiple pictures of a younger Beaufort with a serious widow's peak and the same can-opener nose.

"Fuck me," I said loud enough to get a cautionary "Seamus, your language," from downstairs.

I HAD PROMISED MEGAN BEACH time after lunch while Mom performed a darts exhibition fund raiser at some club or the other at The Landings on Skidaway Island. The day had warmed into the mid-seventies, but we still found a spot with no one else around. Without any wind to face into, seagulls were pointed every which way. Their occasional squabbles were the only thing to mar the background sound of lazy waves lapping the sand.

I had not promised Megan I wouldn't meet someone. An off-duty Detective Sergeant Brittney Issa found us ensconced on the sand two streets north of the pier. Megan was playacting a story with plastic people and horses and dinosaurs. She'd piled sand into loose hills surrounding a fort and was in the process of filling its moat with water.

I rose at Issa's approach. "Thanks for coming on short notice." With a swift glance, I appreciated her toned legs and red bikini bottom. A diaphanous white cover-up only partially hid the top half of the bikini. I was getting the impression her favorite color was red. Dark round sunglasses dominated her face, which was shaded by a wide straw hat.

She dropped her bag next to the towels I'd laid on the sand, motioned me down to the blanket, and sat down next to me—close next to me. "It's my free day. A date, Seamus, does not include a six-year old chaperone." She pointed to Megan playing at the ocean's edge. "What's up?"

Megan ran up and dumped another bucketful of saltwater into her moat.

"Hi, Megan. Those are great looking dinos. Do they have names?"

Megan described in detail how she had acquired each one, and their names, and who was related to whom. "Grampa Seamus says I can take them on the plane tonight."

"You're going home tonight?" Issa gave me a questioning glance.

"Okay, Pumpkin, your moat needs more water, and we need to have some adult talk." Megan hurried to the water, bucket swinging, scattering a group of beggar seagulls who had wandered near to see if we had anything of interest.

I scanned the beach to make sure no one was close enough to bother Megan. By the time I returned my attention to Issa, she was leaning on one elbow, the focus of her shrewd eyes on me. "What gives?" she said.

"I need your help to run a sting operation." I fessed up to my stupidity falling for Fake Beaufort. "Right now, all you can get him on is trespassing and maybe some malicious mischief or the like. The ten grand is technically still mine, provided Fake Beaufort deposited it into a lawyer's legitimate escrow account."

"But if the lawyer's involved, you're out ten large ones."

"If they steal it, but that's chump change. There's a cool million on the line. They won't hotfoot it for a measly ten grand. We need to let it run. Pretend I have no clue I'm getting scammed. I complete the deal, and you follow Fake Beaufort until he deposits the check. It gives us time to learn if the lawyer is complicit in the scam or is being used. Plus, he has a key to the condo. Who gave it to him? That's another cog."

"Wait a minute, the lawyer has a key to the condo?"

"Fake Beaufort." I mentally replayed my last statement. "Misplaced modifier or something. Sorry."

"Let's back up. Do you think this involves the stolen car ring? Or your mother's stolen phone?"

"Has nothing to do with Mom's cell phone because that was stolen before I even knew the apartment was for sale. I suppose the scam could be linked to the stolen car ring. That doesn't exactly make sense. Other than being illegal, there's nothing in common. Is there?"

"You have a plan. Spill."

"This will work. We'll need permission from the

real Andrew Russell Beaufort. We need him not to interfere and to be prepared to swear he's the true owner, et cetera."

"Assume he agrees, then what?"

"I complete the transaction. You nab the scum. We figure out who else is in the network. If your department permits, I can offer my expertise to evaluate the guy's past banking and investment records and see if he's done this before."

"This is above my pay grade. Make me understand your motivation before I stick my neck out bringing this to the captain."

"You know that catching financial criminals is what I do—did, anyway. Let's roll up this operation and reduce Tybee crime. I still plan to buy here, and I want the place clean of flotsam and jetsam."

She brushed away some sand. I considered offering to help, but figured she had switched to business mode, so I kept my suggestion to myself.

"Why call me on my day off? Why not bring this to the station?"

"I'll let you choose," I said. "Door one: you've shown your trust in me and I wanted to repay you. Door two: I wasn't going to cheat Megan from her last day at the beach since I was sending her home early. Door three: I can't stop thinking about our kiss."

For the first time, I witnessed how angelic her face looked in full smile. "Thank you for number one, but it is clearly I who owe you. I believe number two." She waved toward Megan, who was bringing more moat water. "We can revisit number three, but right now I need to convince the Captain that your plan will work."

* * *

THAT EVENING THE RENTAL HOUSE felt empty without Megan. To burn off the anxiety of not knowing what was going on, I went for a walk and found myself on the beach in front of the condo I had thought I would buy. Regret sat on my shoulders. Our time on Tybee was nearing an end. Instead of a carefree vacation and finding a condo to purchase, I'd stressed out my granddaughter by forcing her quick departure, and I had found no other condo I wanted.

Megan would quickly recover, and I was sure she would fondly remember the time here. My problem was that this condo had grown on me like an infatuation for a married woman whose positive attributes grew mythic the more unattainable she became.

My cell phone's ring brought me out of the funk. Unknown local number.

"Sorry for the delay," Issa responded to my cautious hello. "The Captain needed to check you out with some departments you worked for. Good news: he heard strong praise. Bad news: he still has some requirements. Good news: the real Mr. Beaufort is a sweetheart. Couldn't thank us enough for discovering the scam and wants to prosecute to the fullest extent of the law. He'll help any way he can. He was even willing to fly down to swear out a complaint."

"Requirements?" I said, focusing on the bad news.

"We need this to go down on Tybee so it stays in our jurisdiction. If the closing is at the lawyer's there's no way we can pull together a joint operation in time."

"I think I can solve that."

"And we'll need you to wear a transmitter."

"What else?"

"Chief wants to know who this guy is in case something happens so we can get a warrant for his arrest. Not that we'll lose him, but . . ."

"The inspection is set for tomorrow. I can 'borrow' something from the house that'll have his prints."

"Tainted evidence. We'd need a warrant, which we might be able to get. What time's your inspection?"

"I don't like it. Too many people hear of the sting and word leaks. Do a conference call with the real Mr. Beaufort and have him give permission for me to remove something from his condo. If I choose something with the fake Beaufort's fingerprints, we're cool. Right?"

She launched the opening salvos of what I feared was a War and Peace length dissertation on lawyers and evidence rules.

I interrupted. "I see your point. Give me Beaufort's number, and I'll get him to agree. You guys haven't deputized me. Anything I bring to you will just be a citizen doing his duty."

"Good luck, Citizen McCree."

Day 5, Friday

Nerves brought me to the condo early for my meeting with the inspector. Instead of waiting in the car, I photographed the exterior, ending at the private path to the beach. I kicked off my shoes and walked circles on the deserted sand. With each step, cold quartz particles worked their way between my toes, abrading them. In the flat calm ocean, a pod of four dolphins fished for breakfast, their sleek bodies so perfectly suited for the sea. Now was not the time to wonder about my place on earth. I had work to do. The inspector arrived at the appointed time. Mother would be proud of him.

Fake Beaufort retreated to the deck while I followed the inspector around, listening to his commentary and snapping pictures to record everything in the house and on the walls.

We were in and out of the house, so I kept my jacket on. In one pocket I had a cotton glove and a baggie. Real Beaufort assured me that any dishes or cutlery not stored had been used since he last left. In the master bathroom, Fake Beaufort had a water glass by the sink. Lip smudges suggested he had used it to rinse his mouth or take bedtime pills. Perfect for fingerprints and DNA.

The inspector went to look at the third-floor balcony, and I used the opportunity to slip on the glove, place the glass in the baggie, and stash everything back in the pocket. The next time we went outside, I stowed my jacket in the car. Asking Fake Beaufort if I could get a drink of water earned me access to the kitchen cabinets, where I found the same glasses. I wandered with my filled glass to the third floor, dumped the water in the sink, and left the glass on the counter.

The inspector gave me a verbal report: roof still had twenty years on it (or, he joked, one category three hurricane), I should change the balcony railing from horizontal to vertical, the beginnings of cracks in the garage floor suggested minor settling— something to watch to make sure it doesn't worsen. Nothing to stop the deal. He'd get the written report to me on Monday.

I joined Fake Beaufort on the deck. "Good news on the inspection. I wonder if we can convince TBI to allow us to do the closing at their place. Let the lawyer come to us, right? We're paying him. That way I can do the last walk through inspection just before we close, and after we sign our deal, I can work with them on a rental agreement."

He talked with Courtney Souchi, the sales director at the rental agency, making it sound like he was the one who had convinced me to use them, and made his ask. She'd be delighted to reserve the conference room from one to two on Wednesday. He simply told the lawyer that's where the closing would be. No argument there, either.

"One last thing," he said. "I haven't worked with this lawyer before, and I don't know if you should make out the cashier's check to the same escrow account and he makes the disbursements or whether it goes directly to me."

"Good question." I bet myself that I knew what he would suggest.

His face expressed concentration and he snapped his finger, as though something had just occurred to him. "If you make it cash, we're covered either way."

After his impressive performance, ending with the inclusion of me as part of the group "covered," I felt obligated to agree to his plan. Mental note: be very careful not to underestimate him.

Closing Day

THE INTERVENING DAYS FLEW BY. Everything seemed to be in place for the Wednesday closing. In case Fake Beaufort's plan was to mug me and steal the cashier's check made out to cash at the condo when we did the final walk through, I left the check with Mom and dropped her at the library to keep her safe until we sprang the trap. I was wired up and transmitting. Show time.

Fake Beaufort waited under the awning, avoiding the afternoon rain, and watched me park in the condo's driveway. He had no interest in accompanying me on my walk around the exterior of the building. I rounded the corner to the ocean side and startled a flock of grackles into squawking flight across the sand dunes. Even with rain resounding on the metal roof, I could hear the thrum of ocean waves on sand. Sniffing the tang of ocean salt caused a wave of disappointment to wash over me. I tuned into the piece I was humming. Joni Mitchell reminding me I didn't know what I had 'til it was gone. Would Real Beaufort entertain an offer?

Focus on the task at hand, Seamus.

With Fake Beaufort tagging along, I systematically explored the garage, first, second, and third floors. I opened cabinet doors, peeked in closets, opened bureau drawers, and ran the hot water from a faucet.

Clothes were no longer present, and the telescope was gone. Everything else was where I expected it to be, including—if the art expert to whom I had emailed pictures of the wall hangings was correct—fifty thousand dollars' worth of artwork.

The con artist was charming. If he was nervous, I couldn't tell. I hoped he could say the same about me, although my stomach churned and burned with acid, and my mouth still stung from the reflux of the piece of dry toast I had choked down for lunch. "Quick question," I said at the end of my inspection. "When do I pay you for the furnishings?" I had convinced the police to let me give him a chance to take that money now, so even if the closing fell through, we'd nail him for one count of grand larceny. "I brought cash. That was our agreement, right? Hundreds fresh from the bank." Old bills whose serial numbers we'd recorded, although I neglected to share that detail with him.

"Oh, sure. Great."

I pulled the envelope from my jacket pocket, giving him a good look at the promised twenty-five Ben Franklins paper-clipped together. "I made up a little bill of sale." I signed and dated the paper and handed him the pen and paper. He scanned it, signed A. Beaufort, and slid it to me. He agreed to my counting of the hundreds.

"Terrific," I said and meant it. Fake Beaufort was going down for sure. "I have the cashier's check locked up in a courier case. I'll pick it up and meet you at the closing. My mother can't wait to move in this afternoon."

* * *

I HUNG MY DRIPPING RAIN jacket on the coat tree in reception and followed Courtney Souchi into a chilly TBI Real Estate Management conference room. Someone else must have thought it was chilly because a penguin had joined the beach decorations. I was the only one in short sleeves. I'd have to keep in mind that the south tended to over air-condition.

Fake Beaufort was sipping an iced tea and talking to a guy dressed in a slightly rumpled suit. I guessed him to be the lawyer and offered my hand to introduce myself. "I'm the buyer, Seamus McCree. You must be Mr. Prz . . ." My nerves were jangled and I couldn't remember how to pronounce Przybylski.

"It's a mouthful, which is why I prefer people just call me Bill. I've received from your counsel copies of the title search and your title insurance." He handed me a flapped folder. "Once we're done signing documents, I'll make you a copy of the sales agreement. You'll receive the proof of title directly from the County in a couple of weeks. I want to confirm that you're making a cash purchase free of any liens, mortgages, or other encumbrances?"

We all sat and went through the normal closing routine. Przybylski was organized, with copies of the papers for himself, me, and Fake Beaufort. I insisted on reading the small print, which I'd do in a real closing. Przybylski, Fake Beaufort, and Courtney talked weather, planned summer vacations, and whatnot. Courtney seemed slightly hyper compared to the first time I'd met her. Przybylski and Fake Beaufort seemed normal.

"And now, the final payment?" Przybylski looked at me.

I unlocked the courier case and pulled the cashier's check from a dark blue envelope.

Przybylski compared its value to the records in front of him. "Exactly correct. Made out to cash?"

With a flash of inspiration, I accepted the blame to ease any concerns Fake Beaufort might be experiencing. "I wasn't sure exactly how to do it while I was at the bank, and I figured cash would work for everyone."

The lawyer furrowed his brow and gave a short shrug. "Now, Mr. Beaufort, if you'll sign the sales agreement here and date there." He waited for the signatures and continued. "One last thing. The closing documentation includes a list of the items I have or will pay on your behalf, including recording fees and my own compensation. If that's satisfactory with you, I'll write you a check to represent the remaining amount of the deposit."

All as it should be, I thought. These guys are better than good. If I didn't know this was a con, nothing in what happened would have clued me in. Fake Beaufort agreed to the fees, and Przybylski used an old fashioned three-check per page with carbon copies book to write the check. Beaufort shoved it in the same pocket he had stored the cash I'd given him for the condo contents.

"You know," I said, "I should have made a copy of the cashier's check for my records." I faced Courtney and, already knowing it was around the corner behind the conference room, I asked, "You have a copier?"

She hopped up from her seat by the door. "Oh, I can make copies. And Seamus, once we excuse these gentlemen, we have contracts ready for you." She tapped a pile of papers in front of her. "I might even have your first rental lined up!"

Taking the check from Przybylski, I followed Courtney. No way I'd let a crucial step be handled by someone else. The machine flashed and hummed and produced a copy, which I kept, leaving her the original. Now I wanted to give the conspirators, whoever they might be, a little space. "Men's room?"

When I returned to the conference room, Przybylski and Fake Beaufort were standing, chatting. Beaufort extended his hand and we shook. "Congratulations. I hope you enjoy your new place on Tybee." His face darkened in concern. "Where's the check?"

"With Courtney? I made a copy and hit the men's room." I waved the copy of the check in front of them. "Let me see." I hurried into the rear. No Courtney. I called her name and from a cubicle came a voice, "She just left."

"Courtney stole the check," I said, to make sure Detective Sergeant Issa and crew understood the situation. I spotted an exit sign and followed a hall to the back door, where I stuck my head into a fine mist. Six parking spaces lined the back of the building. Five were taken; one showed a dry outline of where a car had been parked. "Rear exit. Left in a car."

Przybylski and Fake Beaufort had followed my voice outside. A sheen of sweat covered Beaufort's face, his hands shook the door as he held it open.

"She stole it?" Przybylski sounded incredulous. "But it's worthless to her."

Fake Beaufort was so angry or upset he couldn't speak. I'd bet Courtney absconding with the check was not part of his plan, and I had inadvertently given her the opportunity. " 'Fraid not," I said. "Remember, it's made out to cash."

"That was stupid," Przybylski said. "Why did you do that?" He pulled a cell phone from his suit coat pocket.

"I'll catch the bitch." Fake Beaufort dug keys from his pocket, grabbed the lawyer's phone, and hopped into his car before we could react. "No cops," he yelled through the closed windows. He reversed out of the parking spot with such acceleration that on the slick driveway he almost slid into the adjacent cars.

"What the hell?" Przybylski said.

"You think they're in this together?" I watched his reaction closely. He didn't seem nervous, or scared, or anything other than confused. Either he was a great actor, or he had no clue about the scam. His mouth opened and closed. Finally, he said, "We need to call the police."

I knew the police were fully aware of the situation from listening to my transmitter, but I thought it imprudent to inform the lawyer. What I didn't know was if they had followed Courtney or if she had given them the slip.

Inside, I found the person attached to the voice from the cubicle, a part-time employee who was putting together the cleaning schedule for the next month. I handed her phone to Przybylski, and he reported the theft to the local 911 operator.

While we waited for the police, I steered the lawyer to the conference room and sat him down before he collapsed. I poured him another iced tea. "You probably want something stronger, but drink this. How'd you meet Beaufort?"

He tipped the chair and closed his eyes. "He called my office, what . . . a week, ten days ago?" He swallowed the ice tea the wrong way and went into a coughing fit. Once he could breathe again he asked, "Why the hell did you make the cashier's check out to cash? Criminy. He took possession, right? I'm not on the hook for this, right?"

My phone buzzed with a text message from Issa. *Out front now!*

"Spill. What happened?" Mom asked when I picked her up at the library on the way to a later-than-intended dinner the night of the closing.

"They picked them both up at a checkpoint they had to go through to leave the island. The police hadn't told me, but the fingerprints I lifted led them to a trail of scams in Florida and Arizona. Places with lots of snowbirds. Same M.O. He seduces an employee at a rental agency to get access to vacant condos. He moves in and runs the scam, promising afterward to take the woman with him to a place he has in the Caribbean. He's always disappeared and left them holding the bag."

"Has he confessed?"

"He first claimed entrapment. Said it was all my idea. That didn't fly, so he tried blaming Courtney.

She's singing like a jilted lover. Each thinks the other absconded with a good cashier's check. Neither one has realized I had set it up with my bank to use special paper. When I copied the check, the photocopier's UV light triggered a reaction that in a few minutes caused VOID to materialize across the original."

"And the lawyer wasn't involved."

"I feel sorry for him. I suggested he take whatever hard costs he had incurred, not counting his time, from the ten-thousand-dollar earnest money. It seemed fair. I could have warned him of the scam and didn't."

"Anyone tell you that your mother raised a soft touch?"

No one was quite like her. I was glad she was mine and I was hers. I patted her head in appreciation.

In pushing my hand away, she knocked off her sunglasses. Her attempt to retrieve them pushed them beyond her reach. "I'll get them later," she said.

I found the last spot in Mom's favorite pizza place's parking lot. Mom brought the seat all the way forward, opened the back door, and fished for her glasses. "Oh damn," she said.

"Good thing Megan isn't around to hear you. What?"

She held up her lost cell phone. "Look what I found."

IT WAS NEARLY NINE BY the time we finished dinner, and I was tired. I'd had a couple of beers with the pizza. Three, actually, spaced over an hour and a half.

The combination made me slow to react to Mom's, "There's Megan's mystery man."

I jammed on the brakes and pulled to the curb. My mother was twisting in her seat, staring down Sixth Street—the same place Megan had seen the guy before.

"No, Seamus," my mother shouted at my back. I was already out the door and running toward Sixth. At the corner, I spotted a man in a hoodie walking rapidly down the street. His gait looked familiar. I sprinted after him, my feet slapping hard on the pavement, the reverberations shooting pains up my shins.

The sound must have alerted him because he stopped and turned around. Instead of running, he held his ground. His puzzled expression grew into a smile.

And now that I was close to him, I realized I had no idea how to approach this conversation. This guy, or any guy for that matter, had not stolen my mother's cell phone, although he, or someone who wore a hoodie, had pawed through our bags at the beach and frightened Megan.

I panted to a halt a few feet away from him. He was late teens, early twenties, with a patchy goatee and wide nose. He resembled Megan's guy, but I needed to be cool. Right!

"Sorry to run after you," I said between breaths. "My granddaughter thinks you were on the beach and hovered over her and later looked through our beach bags. She's scared and so . . ."

"Mr. McCree, right?"

Proof he'd been following me. "And you are?"

"Sorry." He held out his hand. "Karl Obendorf. Hey man, I didn't mean to scare the kid. I was trying to work up the nerve to introduce myself—I don't mean—not to her—I'm not a pervert or anything."

He shifted from foot to foot, edgy, but with a dry, firm handshake. I figured not giving him an easy escape from the possible pervert hole he had dug himself was the best way to satisfy my curiosity about why he wanted to introduce himself to me. It's not like I was famous or delivering a Publishers Clearing House check.

He indulged in a long sigh. "Let me try this again. I am a *huge* fan of your mother's. I've read and heard all about her exhibitions and the money she collects for charity and everything. I even watched some YouTube videos of her events, and I've watched all her instructional videos. I just love her, ya know? And when I saw her on the beach?" His high voice rose into a question. "I wasn't sure it was her. You know? I mean, what are the chances, right? That Trudy McCree, darts legend, was on my beach? I wanted to meet her, but if it wasn't her, I'd look like a fool."

As was I to think this was about me. *Oh, Seamus, will you never learn?*

He swiped at his sweating forehead with the heel of his hand. "I walked away and circled back. Mrs. McCree was gone, but you and the kid were there. I thought I'd ask her name. If it was McCree, I'd know I was right. I'm sucking up enough nerve to speak and she's building this awesome castle and talking to fairies and pretend friends. And I realized how stupid my idea was. I mean, she shouldn't talk to strangers, right?"

"I'm glad she listened to us."

"Right. That's good. Anyway, I didn't say anything to her, and by the time I came up with an approach that didn't make me look stupid, I saw you and the girl were on the flats. If I could find an ID, then I'd know for sure. Talk about stupid! I made it worse by panicking when I realized you were watching me."

"But you figured out we're the McCrees."

"Yeah, right, I like followed you and asked around, see. But I couldn't get up my nerve to knock on your door. I mean, how weird is that, the darts paparazzi?"

I followed his attention and spotted my mother walking down the sidewalk.

"Before my mother gets here, do you have an ID I can see?"

"Yeah. Sure, man." He pulled his driver's license from his wallet. Karl J. Obendorf, aged twenty-one, lived right on Sixth Street, which explained how he had disappeared when I had tried to catch up to him a few days earlier.

"I'm big time into darts. Even got a board inked on my leg." He rotated his calf so I could see the tat.

What Megan thought was an elongated spider with a red eye and a fish tail was a dart scoring a bullseye. The "fish tail" was the dart's fins.

Mom had stopped a half-block away, a finger posed on her phone. I waved her toward us. I said under my breath to Karl, "If I were you, I'd start with an apology to The Legend and take it from there."

"I hear you, man. I sure didn't mean to spook the kid, and I'm sorry I alarmed you the other day."

I had no clue what he was talking about and pulled

my stupid response from my toolbox of tricks. Putting on a puzzled expression, I said, "How so?"

"Following you? I tried doing it on foot to see where you lived. Maybe I'd work up enough nerve to knock on your door. But you were driving, and I never found out exactly where you were staying. Then I spotted your car last week. When you caught me following you at Fort Pulaski and took my picture, I should have stopped and introduced myself then. But I panicked again. I didn't want you thinking I was a stalker, or something."

Aha! "The Land Cruiser?"

"Yeah. Delivering cars for people to their mechanic is a great part-time gig while finishing college. There was a snafu and I had to hold onto the SUV until I got a new delivery address. I'm not supposed to use them for personal stuff. You won't rat me out, right? No harm, no foul."

Unfortunately for my new BFF, the police thought stolen cars were a foul, and Karl knew where the setup had been relocated. Mom sidled up to me, keeping me between herself and Karl.

"A fan of yours. He thinks you're a legend." I stepped to one side. "Will you excuse me? I need to make a call."

Karl enthused. Mom demurred. I pressed the speed dial for Issa's cell phone. "It's Seamus. Sixth Street by the beach. ASAP. Make it official, but no lights. You can thank me later."

Author's Note

THIS NOVELLA WAS BIRTHED AS part of a project I started in 2016 to publish a collection of four novellas, each by a different author, all set in the Lowcountry of the Southeastern United States. "Low Tide at Tybee" was my contribution to the collection, which is titled *Lowcountry Crime: Four Novellas.* In the introduction to that volume, I provided two definitions to provide context:

Lowcountry: That portion of the Southeastern United States characterized by low country, generally flat—whether barrier island, tidal marsh, tidal river valleys, swamps, piney forests, or great cities like Charleston and Savannah.

Crime: An act, forbidden by a public law, that makes the offender liable to punishment by that law.

At the time of its writing, we were wintering in the Savannah area. I thought it would be fun to have Seamus join me down south for a short vacation. Once again, Seamus's desire for relaxation didn't turn out as he expected.

I spent many fine days wandering Tybee's beaches, birdwatching and people-watching. The cover photograph is one I took of sanderlings feeding near its southern tip. I never experienced any crime on Tybee, although I'm sure it exists. If you happen to be in the area, I encourage you to check out the island and see why Seamus liked it so well.

Although I prefer to use real locations whenever I can, I generally create the crooked businesses in my stories, as is the case with the real estate firm.

My name is on the cover and any mistakes are mine. I love to hear from readers. Drop me a note and let me know how you liked the story or that you found a typo so I can correct it for future editions. My email is jmj@jamesmjackson.com.

James M. Jackson
Amasa, Michigan

James M. Jackson authors the Seamus McCree series.

Jim has also published an acclaimed book on contract bridge, *One Trick at a Time: How to start winning at bridge.*

He calls the deep woods of Michigan's Upper Peninsula home. You can find out more about Jim or sign up for his Readers Group newsletter at his website, https://jamesmjackson.com.